EMBRACE THE WILD

EMBRACE THE WILD

Caris Roane

Formatting and cover by Bella Media Management.

ISBN-13: 978-1512114348

THE BLOOD ROSE SERIES
BOOK SIX

EMBRACE THE WILD

CARIS ROANE

Dear Reader,

Welcome to the sixth installment of the Blood Rose Series, EMBRACE THE WILD. In this book, Mastyr Malik chases the powerful fae, Willow, through the forests, his desire for her close to an obsession. Willow in turn can't stop lusting for the vampire who rules all of Ashleaf Realm. But where can their two-year-long flirtation go when each is sworn to serve their realm above all else?

For two-hundred-years he's lived a solitary existence until a beautiful fae, with enormous power, disrupts his world…

Mastyr Vampire Malik has only one goal: to serve the realm he loves. Battling both the dreaded Invictus wraith-pairs and an element in Ashleaf Realm that wants all innocent wraiths dead, Malik can't afford to get distracted. But Willow has already become an obsession as he lusts for the powerful fae whose blood he craves. In turn, Willow has her own duties to attend to as the Protector of a large, vulnerable wraith colony. Without her shield, the innocent wraiths will be caught by the malevolent Society, a group intent on killing all wraiths and half-breeds. But her drive toward Malik, her need to be with him, to feed him, overrides her rational mind. Passion storms through her life, changing everything. But at what cost to herself, to Malik, to the entire Realm?

Enjoy!

Caris Roane

Chapter One

Willow swam in a large forest pool, trying to ignore the vampire watching her from deep in the woods. As she swept each arm through the water and kicked her feet, she felt his attention like a soft drag on her body, slowing her down and making her want things from him she shouldn't want.

Of course she knew who he was; she'd known him since she could remember. He was Mastyr Malik, ruler of Ashleaf Realm for two hundred years, a warrior and a man of great worth, always willing to lay down his life for his fellow realm-folk.

For her, he'd become the standard by which she measured all men, especially since he fought on behalf of wraith civil rights every night of his life, protecting the tens of thousands of half-breeds who lived in Ashleaf Realm.

No other mastyr before him had done so.

Every few days for the past two years, Malik would seek her out at the end of his nightly patrols with his Vampire Guard, a half hour or so before dawn. And she made it a point to be at her favorite waterfall, swimming, her clothes left on the ground.

She'd been without a man for way too long, decades in fact because she'd vowed never to let herself get distracted from her duties. What she couldn't deny, however, was that over the past two years since her encounters with Malik had begun, she'd grown to crave her brief time with him.

Even as she pulled through the water, her body felt heated and unsettled — needy. At times, her desire for the mastyr distracted her almost beyond reason and still she allowed herself this moment of perfect erotic sensation. She would pleasure herself later with the memory of what would soon follow, even though she forbade herself to touch Malik or even to engage in conversation with him. She risked too much as it was.

She felt his desire though, and could smell his powerful mating scent, very much like the richest parts of the forest. That Malik took pleasure in watching her swim made her feel as though she provided him a small service. She knew what he suffered, and not just the chronic blood-starvation that all mastyr vampires of the Nine Realms suffered, but because she knew he bore the concerns of his realm heavily on his shoulders.

Reaching the waterfall end of the natural pool, she flipped over and headed back in the mastyr's direction, floating on her back, stroking toward the opposite bank. She breathed in his rough, wild texture, warrior that he was, so very male.

But she could feel the moment build within her when she'd have to rise naked from the pool and run. He always gave chase and she always ran, knowing that if he ever caught her, she wouldn't be able to restrain herself.

And if she gave herself to Malik, she feared that his entire Realm would be thrown into the worst and most horrific chaos of its long existence.

She wasn't just a wraith-fae half-breed. She also served as the sole Protector of an entire colony of pure wraiths that lived hidden and safe on her land. If it ever became known that so many full-blooded wraiths lived in Ashleaf, those aligned with The Society would come after them, slaughtering to the last living soul.

~ ~ ~

Malik remained cloaked by the deep night shadows of the surrounding forest, knowing that in about three minutes he'd be chasing a very naked woman through a dozen intricate paths.

But he was quickly reaching the point where just watching Willow swim at the base of the waterfall wouldn't be enough. He needed to be with her, to talk to her, to touch her, and do a thousand other things he shouldn't.

The woman's name was Willow and she always ran, and always eluded him. Clearly, she didn't want to be caught. So why did he keep giving chase?

Though he'd long since given up on his rational process having any effect on this obsession, that old saying about insanity and repeated behavior slid through his head. Yet, just once he wanted to hold the powerful elusive fae-female in his arms, maybe sink his fangs and drink until he was Goddess-be-damned satisfied.

He could smell her blood as well, a fresh forest-rain scent, even at a distance of forty feet. He had to pant through a couple of serious stomach-killing cramps just to keep from doubling over. He wanted her blood like no other woman he'd desired in the past century.

His blood-starvation from the time he'd risen to mastyr status two hundred years ago had been his closest friend and one he cursed nightly. Though he had a stable of faithful and extremely reliable *doneuses* who fed him twice a day, he still suffered as though he never tapped a vein.

The *mastyr* curse was a real bitch.

But with that curse came power and lots of it, and more than other vampires in Ashleaf Realm.

Yet, he still couldn't catch the quick-footed fae. Each time she scurried down intricate forest paths, he followed suit, putting on as much of his renowned vampire speed as he could, but he never quite caught up.

Her track might be different each time, but the end was always the same; she would reach the vine-shrouded gate to her land and simply vanish. How many times had he stood near the massive tangle of vines, feeling her presence, calling to her, begging her to show herself, but without ever having her respond? He wasn't sure, but somehow he believed she had a connection to those vines, that they gave her shelter.

Once he'd actually tried to force her hand, waiting until the break of dawn before heading home. But all he'd gotten for his trouble were a few extremely painful sunlight-blisters, having cut it that close to sunrise.

But she hadn't revealed herself to him. Not even then.

For a few days after each chase, he would resolve never to return to her. However, his need for what she possessed in her veins called to him repeatedly so that with hope raging in his chest, he would find his way back to this exact pool and her beautiful, naked body moving through the water.

So here he was … again … hoping against any rational possibility that tonight would be different. Maybe she'd stumble, and he'd catch her. Or maybe he'd find just enough additional power to capture her at last. Then he would hold her and ease her head to just the right angle, exposing her long, beautiful throat and pulsing vein.

A vampire could only hope.

She swam easily in the water, long strokes from the waterfall at one end, to the other where ferns abounded. She hummed a soft folk tune now, something that sounded fae, something she would accompany with a lyre.

Even as she hummed, he felt that her entire being was focused on something else, something other than the water or the song, or plying her arms and kicking her feet, or even on him. This he always felt as well, as though her mind was fixed on an object he didn't understand.

He'd known Willow since her parents had died as a result of The Society, a group bent on ridding Ashleaf Realm of all wraiths and half-breeds. Willow was one-quarter wraith and her mother, a lovely fae-wraith, had been slaughtered by The Society.

Willow's father had died as a result of grief-insanity. He'd lashed out, trying to find his wife's killers, but ended up facing off with Malik and his Vampire Guard. The tall full-fae man, an honorable teacher of ancient history at Ashleaf University, had died while holding an innocent troll hostage, a knife to his neck, blood flowing from the troll's throat.

Willow had been thirteen at the time, almost seventy years ago now. He'd known her back then, and that Alexandra the Bad, the most powerful fae in the Ashleaf Guild, had shortly afterward sent Willow secretly to live with a family in the far north. She'd been given a new identity in order to keep her safe from The Society.

Then two years ago, he'd seen Willow in the market town of Cherry Hollow. He hadn't known who she was at the time, not having seen her in decades. But he was drawn to her auburn hair and soft hazel eyes, as well as an ethereal, almost otherworld quality she carried with her.

He'd called out to her, but she'd disappeared into the forest. He'd given chase that very night, his interest developing quickly into a profound desire.

And here he was, watching her do laps in a pool, listening to the sound of the waterfall and smelling the sweet forest scent of her blood until the muscles of his thighs twitched.

He desired this woman as though she was rain to his storm.

And from the scent that rose from the water, he knew she felt the same way and that she was fully aware of his presence. But why wouldn't she come to him? Why did she run when he drew near? Why wouldn't she even talk to him?

Dawn wasn't far away now and he had to make his move soon, or he'd end up blistered by the time he made it back to his house some thirty miles to the south.

He'd patrolled Ashleaf through the night with his Vampire Guard, hunting for sign of the enemy, the dreaded Invictus wraith-pairs. But his realm was mercifully quiet and he'd sent his Guard home for the night.

The time had come.

And at nearly the same moment that he decided to move, as though somehow intuiting his intentions, she levitated out of the pool and started to dry off with her towel. He nearly passed out at the sight of her exquisite and completely naked body.

"Willow," he called softly. "Don't run this time. I just want to talk."

She lifted her head, paused for about a split-second to meet his gaze, then spun around and took off. She half-ran, half-levitated, shifting side-to-side to avoid branches and thorny vines as she headed up a north trail.

He flew after her, his three hundred years of living in Ashleaf Realm equal to her deft maneuvers. She sped over waterfalls and down streams and gullies, her nakedness a creamy flash in the night.

The whole time, the scent of her desire trailed after her, letting him know exactly what these encounters meant to her.

Yet he knew so damn little about the woman as she hit a path to the west that veered quickly to the south. Her strategy might change, but she always led him back to that enormous vine-shrouded arbor above the gate to her property. If he didn't catch her, she'd disappear into the vines, dawn would come way too soon, and he'd have to leave yet again without capturing his prize.

On he sped, sometimes losing sight of her because she was so fast. Even as he reached a fork with several paths, he only had to sniff the air to know which route to take.

He ate up the few miles, sweating furiously in his Guardsmen leather coat despite it was sleeveless. But he wouldn't have stopped for the world.

He reached for her telepathically, yet couldn't connect because the woman could block him. Exactly how much power did this fae hold? Possibly more than even Alexandra the Bad, the leader of the Ashleaf Fae Guild.

As her gate loomed, he started closing in. She'd grown fatigued. Part of her energy was still focused elsewhere as he gave chase. He didn't understand what she was concentrating on so heavily.

If only she'd just talk to him; he had so many questions.

He was within fifteen feet … ten … sweet Goddess, only three feet, but there was the damn vine-covered arbor and gate, the place she would disappear. If she reached it, he'd be unable to find her.

He reached out, put on some speed and his fingers trailed down her red hair, half-dry now from running.

But she ran straight into the vines and like at least three dozen times before, she simply vanished.

He flew over the gate to the other side, but he knew she wouldn't be there. Was she really somewhere inside the vines? How was that even possible? Yet, she had to be because he could smell her and she was close.

"Willow, I must talk to you. I don't mean you any harm. I promise you. Won't you speak to me, just once?"

~ ~ ~

Hidden safely within the cocoon of the vines and her hands wrapped around two thick stems, Willow breathed hard.

Malik. Dear sweet Goddess. Malik.

His name was a mantra within her mind, something she called to over and over. But he never heard her. She would never let him hear her need, her desperation, her longing for him.

Did she want to speak to him, even just once?

Yes, yes, yes.

And he was so close; she could have touched him. Sweat poured down his face and he wiped it away with the sleeve of the woven shirt he wore, the traditional shirt of all Vampire Guardsmen.

"Willow, please." His deep voice reached into her chest and squeezed her heart. "Give me a chance. There's something here between us, something important, maybe even realm-based. But how can we figure this out, if you won't even talk to me?"

The plaintive sound of his words clawed at her soul, but she closed her eyes and shored up her resistance to him. He didn't know, couldn't know, that she longed to give in, that she wanted more than anything to show herself and to tell him why she couldn't open up to him.

But she was sworn to secrecy and couldn't violate her vows. So many wraiths depended on her.

The minutes wore on and because dawn was so close, she knew he had to leave, had to return to his home in order to avoid the sun. Her situation wasn't much different. As a fae, she needed to be inside during the daylight hours.

But if caught outside, she could hide herself in the vines, a sacred power she'd gleaned from the fae Protector before her.

If only she could share the truth with Malik, she could end this absurd chase through the forest with him. Yet, even as this thought ran through her head, she knew she didn't want Malik to ever stop giving chase. She'd lived such a solitary life for decades that just having him near had added a layer of joy to her existence she never wanted to give up.

Almost two years ago now, she'd seen him on market day in Cherry Hollow, one of Ashleaf's largest towns. She'd gone there cloaked with a fae charm so that anyone who saw her wouldn't pay her the smallest attention. She went often to various towns and villages throughout Ashleaf to buy her food and other supplies, though hidden behind her spells.

But on this night, she'd seen Malik outside a tavern, standing with several of his Guardsmen across from a pen of goats for sale. They were each having a pint, relaxing. Confident that neither he nor his Guardsmen would be able to see through her charm, she allowed herself to watch Malik and his men. She'd enjoyed just listening to the occasional burst of male laughter.

Then Malik had laughed at something one of his lieutenants had said, and something inside Willow's chest had started to ache. That smile had sent hooks deep into her heart, especially since she knew for a certainty that Malik rarely smiled, that a great sadness ruled his life. He was a thoroughly responsible ruler who took his job as seriously as she took her own. And he faced challenges within his realm that she honestly didn't know how he bore as well as he did.

How long she'd stood like that just staring at him she didn't know. But she took the time to memorize his strong cheekbones and thickly arched brows, his large, brown eyes. He looked like a man who could have starred in some of the Hollywood movies she liked to watch. He was that attractive.

She knew a lot about him as well, and about his constant effort to bring The Society under control.

When Malik had taken over as Mastyr of Ashleaf over two hundred years ago, he'd instituted a great number of laws meant to protect the half-breed population of the realm. But Mastyr Axton, who Malik had supplanted, was believed to have created The Society that same year. Despite the laws making it illegal to vilify, maim, or murder wraiths or half-breeds, The Society had set about the genocidal task in secret, year after year, working through the horribly effective method of small cells to kill the innocent.

Mastyr Axton was a nightmare no one had been able to get rid of legally. In public, he denounced The Society, but had a huge following because he wanted to restore the old ways. In other words, he wanted all wraiths and half-breeds dead without ever using those particular words.

Axton was the consummate hypocrite and liar.

Malik, on the other hand, had won her full support from the moment she learned that he'd been the one to make it a crime to hurt wraiths or their relatives.

But as she stood at the edge of the town of Cherry Hollow that night, longing for the man, Malik had suddenly shifted in her direction and met her gaze.

He'd seen through her charm!

No other mastyr in Ashleaf had ever been able to penetrate one of her spells, not even Axton, the second most powerful vampire in the realm.

She'd almost smiled and waved, until she recalled that she wasn't a normal fae living a normal life in Ashleaf. She was the sole Protector of twenty-thousand souls, who lived in the center of the realm and depended on her for survival.

She'd turned away shortly after and drifted into the forest, her heart downcast, unaware that he'd followed her until he'd called out her name. "Willow. Is that you? Where have you been all these years?"

She'd glanced at him over her shoulder, her heart in her throat. But she couldn't talk to him because the temptation to want more from him than she could possibly give in return would be too great. So she fled, using the power she'd gained over the years, to half-run, half-fly through the forest at a speed not even Malik could quite equal.

She just hadn't expected him to give chase.

He'd almost caught her three times before she reached the safety of the vines at the entrance to her land.

Fortunately, his power had limits and he wasn't able to penetrate the shield the vines created for her.

That night, two years ago, she'd cried herself to sleep, knowing what she was missing and unable to act on her simple desire to talk with him or even to wave at him.

Maybe it was the nature of the chase that had worked each of them up so thoroughly, but if so many people hadn't depended on her for their sheer existence, she would have long since given herself, body and soul, to the Mastyr of Ashleaf Realm.

Now, as she held the vines and watched him leave, her heart ached all over again. She became aware of a heaviness in her chest that she seemed to carry with her all the time now, yet another indication just how much she desired him.

As he finally disappeared, taking off in flight in order to get home before dawn, Willow came back to herself. She needed to get it together and not let her protection of the wraith colony flag.

But at exactly that moment, she felt one of the most powerful wraiths within the colony calling to her telepathically. A sense of fear came through in a way that left Willow panicky.

Illiandra, what's wrong?

A near-breach! Willow, have you not been attending? Your protective shield is under attack.

Now frightened that she might have imperiled so many lives, she released the vines and turned all her energy on the shield that protected the colony. That's when she felt a very specific fae charm burning through the colony's secret entrance.

She had to get over there right away.

Illiandra, apologies. I'm on it.

Illiandra was one of the oldest and wisest wraith leaders of the colony. *Keep me advised.*

Willow flew swiftly the three miles to the tall, granite outcropping that had created a natural barrier to the colony. She could see smoke spiraling into the air.

A short tunnel, hidden behind a thick fall of vines, led through the granite wall straight into the wraith colony. A Guard-sized man stood directly opposite the entrance holding a charm in his hand made up of glowing purple crystals. As he aimed the charm toward the secret opening, the vines smoked and burned.

She knew who he was: Mastyr Axton.

Sweet Goddess, no.

But how had he made it past her property's protective shield? He'd never done so before, which made Willow think that the same fae that had created the purple crystal charm must have helped him move past Willow's spell.

She held her own disguise tight around her then simply melted into the vines. The moment she made direct contact with the thick stems and released her protection vibration, power surged.

At the same time, she aimed a strong burst at Axton's charm. She wasn't a powerful fae for nothing and the singular wave of energy that she released broke the charm's spell. The glow of crystals fizzled, the burning stopped, and Axton cursed long and loud. He looked around as though astonished, then cursed once more.

Because dawn was so close, she wasn't surprised that he simply took to the air and sped southwest high above the forest canopy.

She pathed to Illiandra. *Mastyr Axton somehow came into possession of a powerful, illegal charm. Some of the vines were* destroyed, but as soon as I made contact, I repulsed his attempt. I'm rebuilding the vine-wall now.

Well, done. Illiandra paused, then, *You're unsettled though, aren't you? Did Malik give chase again?*

Yes. She had shared her dilemma with Illiandra, but the wise woman had merely told her to do everything she could to remain strong for the colony.

You must end this, Willow. He's distracting you from the shield. And if Axton has found the entrance to our lands, he'll be back. We're in trouble here, Willow, so please be strong for us. We depend on you.

I know.

The wraith colony was spread out over twenty square miles of land that belonged to Willow on paper. The sheer size of the shield she'd created and supported was one of the reasons she couldn't get distracted. The population had doubled as well in the last forty years, which had made it increasingly difficult for Willow to keep streaming her protective energies.

Willow had fulfilled her duties for decades without too much difficulty. However, in recent years, she seemed to have reached some kind of personal limit. She'd tried repeatedly to tell Illiandra about her concerns, but the wraith had no other answer than to tell Willow 'to be strong'.

Willow wouldn't give up — never that — but she truly feared that something unexpected might happen and she would no longer be able to sustain the protective colony shield.

Illiandra, do you think it's possible that Mastyr Axton knows about the colony?

Impossible, Illiandra responded firmly. *My guess is that he's found a fae willing to help him build charms in order to find wraith-sign. He no doubt stumbled upon the entrance by accident.*

Willow wasn't convinced, but she was tired from the chase and from repulsing Axton's charm. And dawn was on her heels.

She bid Illiandra good-night and headed to her treehouse complex as swiftly as she could.

As she finally fell into bed, her last thought was simple: She had to talk to Malik and end their chasing ritual.

But Sweet Goddess, she didn't want to. Not even a little.

~ ~ ~

"Mastyr, you're hurting me."

Malik heard the woman's voice and somewhere within his mind he knew he needed to ease back on her wrist. Though a full day had passed since he'd last seen Willow, hungry images clouded his head as he once again mentally chased her through the forest. His mind got lost in the erotic images of the smooth, pale skin of her firm buttocks shifting back and forth along the trail, which had him fully aroused.

"Mastyr, you must stop. I'll be bruised to my elbow."

As he continued to suck on the rich vein, his donor's words were a dull noise at the edge of the seductive memories, of needing to catch Willow, of wanting her beneath him, of hungering to pierce her neck and take down her life-force.

"Mastyr, please!" A hand shoved at his head until he finally awoke to his crime.

With a terrible jolt of remorse, he released the wrist of one of his sweetest *doneuses* from whom he'd been feeding. The lovely fae woman, with tears in her brown eyes, held her arm as if in pain.

He'd hurt her.

Sweet Goddess! Not again.

"Miriam, I'm so sorry." Still on his knees, he shifted away from the side of the chair in which she sat. His ass hit the stone tiles of his living room and he held his head in his hands. He was in a painfully aroused state and dammit, he'd become an animal.

He'd promised Miriam he'd keep himself under tight control.

What the hell was wrong with him?

"I'm so sorry, Mastyr Malik, but I can't serve you anymore. My husband was adamant that if this happened again, he wouldn't allow me to come back. I have to resign."

He glanced at her arm, horrified all over again. She'd be black and blue for days unless he did something for her. "Let me call you a healer."

Miriam drew in a deep breath. "That would be best."

Not ready to stand up yet, he shifted to dip his hand into the pocket of his jeans. Pulling out his realm cellphone, he called Alexandra the Bad, who had ruled the Guild in his realm for longer than he'd taken his first breath.

She growled over the phone, somehow knowing exactly what had happened, then stated harshly that she was on her way. Malik knew that when she arrived, she'd deliver a weighty lecture, and one he damn-well deserved.

He then summoned his housekeeper, requesting dewberry tea for Miriam.

His *doneuse* wiped at her eyes.

He was so fucking ashamed. "I'm sorry. Dear sweet Goddess, a thousand apologies."

Miriam huffed a ragged sigh. "Mastyr, if there was any other way."

He lifted a hand. "You don't have to say anything. I was out of control and this is all my fault." He wanted to explain, but what could he say? That he had the hots for a woman who swam naked and disappeared into vines?

But Miriam shook her head. "Please listen to me. I may not be as powerful as the fae in the Ashleaf Guild, but I know that you're suffering in a way you didn't even two years ago. You seem incredibly sad, Mastyr, yet I have this sense that something very realm is upon you, and that whatever possessed your mind just now has a realm source. You shouldn't ignore it."

Malik stared at Miriam for a long moment. Was she right? Was it possible that his obsession with Willow had meaning beyond the deep lust that he experienced? "I'll think on what you've said. I promise."

A few minutes later, Alexandra the Bad assaulted his house.

She was a stout fae with an additional two hundred years on Malik's three centuries. She took one look at Miriam's arm and cast him her deepest scowl, the kind that brought her bushy, porcupine brows into a single, disapproving line. "What the hell have you done, vampire? This is an abomination. Have I not warned you sufficiently?"

"You have, and I have no excuse."

She pinched her lips together. "We will have words, but after."

"Of course."

She turned and focused all her attention on his *doneuse.*

When Alexandra had made all the bruising disappear, she sent Miriam away, then turned the full force of her displeasure on Malik. Compressing her lips, she glared at him. "This is the third time in three weeks. You need to get hold of yourself and don't even think about pulling your 'I'm-the-Mastyr-of-Ashleaf' gremlin shit with me. I dandled you on my knee, Malik, and don't be forgetting that! Stop hurting your *doneuses* or the next time I will report you to the Sidhe Council for abuse. You can count on that."

"There won't be a next time."

"You said that last time."

"I vow to you it will not happen again. I know what I need to do." He'd been avoiding it from the time he first gave Willow chase; he needed to confront the woman who had captured his mind and end this thing between them. It was possible that she'd created some kind of chemistry between them, a charm perhaps. She was, after all, extremely powerful.

But whatever this was, Willow was the cause. And this time, if he had to hunt her down all through the night until she fell exhausted at his feet, he'd force her to explain herself.

"And are you making a vow to the Goddess?" Alexandra asked.

He nodded. "I am."

"Then I suppose I must be satisfied." She narrowed her gaze. "But I can feel your determination, so for the present I will rest in that. I'm counting on you."

"I won't let you down."

After several more glares and at least two 'harrumphs', Alexandra left.

Malik remained by the door for a long moment, a hand pressed to his stomach. Miriam's blood, as fine as any by realm standards, had done little to ease his chronic blood starvation. His stomach cramped but there was nothing to be done about that.

However, the straying of his thoughts all over his most recent experience with Willow had left him with an ache he had to get rid of, and he headed to his bathroom.

He set the jets of his shower on cold, undressed, then stepped in. His skin was so heated that it took the icy feel of the water to bring him down to normal.

But he still needed a release.

Soaping up and leaning a forearm against the tile, he let his thoughts run wild.

Willow.

Sweet Goddess, Willow.

Once more, he saw her auburn hair and milky skin, eyes the color of stormy skies, breasts that made his groin ache. He saw her rising naked from the pool then turning to run.

She moved liked the wind.

He gave chase mentally, while his hand went to work on his cock, pumping fast, his breathing growing rougher by the second.

He knew exactly when he wanted to come. Just a few more seconds as he watched her racing, her narrow waist, full hips, her bottom an invitation like nothing else.

Then there it was. She glanced at him over her shoulder and met his gaze, connecting with him in a way that he felt shot full of fire. He came hard, remembering that look. His balls fired off, sending his seed rocketing, delivering up a rolling series of exquisite pulses.

"Willow," he whispered against the tile and flowing water.

After a moment, when his heart returned to normal, when he heard the wild chattering of the birds in his nearby aviary, he slowly rinsed off and finally left the shower.

He should have felt tremendous relief. Instead, his craving for Willow seemed even more intense. He wanted to touch her, to bury himself between her legs, and to feed from her vein.

By all the elf lords, he was in deep shit.

From a distance, he heard his housekeeper, Francesca, call to him.

Wrapping a towel around his waist, he responded, "What is it?" But his heart sank because his housekeeper only disturbed him in his private quarters when something bad had happened.

"The Society struck again. A murder in Birchingwood. And Mastyr, there were children this time." He heard her voice catch, and his own throat tightened.

Dear Goddess, not children. How would he ever bear it?

~ ~ ~

Well past full-dark, Willow sat cross-legged in her meditation space, one of several isolated rooms in her expansive treehouse complex. Her heart labored, which had been happening a lot lately, especially after Malik gave chase.

She forced her eyes to close as she pressed her thumbs to her middle-fingers and began a soft fae calming chant. Her responsible nature settled deep into her bones once more.

She had to let Malik go. She had to forget about him and her ever-present desire for him, and focus on what was infinitely more important – keeping the wraith-colony from being discovered.

If Mastyr Axton ever found a way in, he'd slaughter everyone: Man, woman, and child. And they were good realm-folk to the last baby wraith.

She ran through one of her favorite centering meditations, *Goddess of all that is love, who created the world of the Nine Realms, the expansive universe above and the blessed earth below, please strengthen me to serve Ashleaf and the colony. And help me to stay focused on the protective shield.*

The simple prayer calmed her mind and solidified her focus. If she continued in this way, she would have no problem supporting the protective shield through the night. She would soon be reaching out to Mastyr Malik as well to arrange for a meeting. Once she ended things between them, she would be able to fully turn her attention to keeping the colony safe.

The wraith community had been part of Ashleaf Realm for more millennia than the current ruling wraiths even knew.

And beneath their cottage-like homes, established in the largest meadowland in Ashleaf, beat the heart of the Nine Realms like a living force that Willow felt even now.

She gained her strength from that beating heart and allowed the vibrations from within the earth to rise and cover her.

She could breathe more easily now.

Suddenly and without warning, however, the image of Malik once more intruded within her mind, but not in the sense of needing or wanting him. Instead, the beating heart of the realm connected her to Malik so that right now she could feel that some kind of terrible despair had overtaken him. Because Malik carried the weight of his realm with him at all times, she knew the sorrow he also bore that half-breeds died so often in Ashleaf.

And she knew without having to be told that more of her kind had died and his sadness became hers.

Her heart reached for him and because she could feel the earth's vibrations, a present-moment vision came to her that brought tears to her eyes. She watched Malik fall to his knees over the bodies of a family of four elves murdered viciously with an axe, the way The Society killed half-breeds. She knew the family because she knew every realm-person in Ashleaf known to have a full-blooded wraith for either a grandparent or a great-grandparent.

Her heart felt bludgeoned as she held the vision within her mind.

Tears now flowed down her face just as they flowed down Malik's.

As one-quarter wraith, she knew the stigma that all half-breeds bore in Ashleaf, and that each realm-person with even a hint of wraith-blood would one day be targeted for extermination by The Society.

She pulled out of the vision and opened her eyes, wiping at her cheeks with the sleeve of her shirt.

She rose from the small space and moved to the window that she'd thrown open for the night. Ashleaf Realm had dozens of night bird species that chattered and called out until dawn. From the thirty foot height of the meditation room, she could see down into the shallow stream at the foot of her oak-based complex. Frogs croaked and some of the larger birds waited to catch a meal near the stream.

She stood there for a long time, just staring down into the stream, listening to the frogs and the chatter of the birds.

Sadness clung to her for a long time as well as thoughts of Mastyr Malik and what it must have been like for him to enter the elves' home. She wished she could ease him and console him at such a terrible time.

Instead, her duties lay elsewhere. She knew what needed to be done, and she made the difficult decision to go immediately to Birchingwood and to finally speak to the man she'd been craving for the past two years.

Chapter Two

Malik walked slowly out of the home of the cobbler elf and his family. He tried to wipe the blood off his hands, but couldn't. He had blood on his leathers, his boots, the bottom edge of his Guardsman coat.

He'd knelt in the spilled blood because there was nothing else he could do. He couldn't bring the family back to life, shore up their horrific wounds, or make the blood disappear. All he could do was kneel, take a moment, honor the dead.

The killer had used an axe.

He leaned against the front porch post, shading his face with his hand. The attack had been incredibly brutal, worse than anything he'd witnessed before, which meant he was sure the family had been tortured.

He'd seen a lot of bloodshed in his life, but the little, twin boys had only been toddlers, maybe two-years-old, if that. Nausea now accompanied his usual stomach cramps, and his mind still wasn't functioning right.

A village woman, a troll and a good neighbor to the family, approached him. She carried a basin of water in her arms, and a rag dangling from her hand. Tears streamed down her cheeks. "We know one day you will make this right, Mastyr, and that you will end The Society forever."

He stared at the tightly compressed ridges of her forehead. He didn't blink as she began wiping the blood from his boots and his Guardsman coat.

As she performed this grief-laden service, he glanced up and down High Street of Birchingwood. He had twenty of his Vampire Guard standing watch at intervals. Many realm-folk wept openly and more than one woman wailed her distress and her grief.

He glanced up at the treehouse level, two and three stories above the ground. Many occupants of the homes up there stood along the rope walkways that led from tree to tree.

Some of the realm-folk wept, some just stared at him in mute horror. Others looked distastefully satisfied by the killing. His realm was completely divided and all because of Mastyr Axton and The Society.

Still struggling to bring his mind to order and absorb what had happened, he didn't know how much more he could take.

An agent from the Realm Investigative Unit was already inside working the crime scene with his forensics team. But they wouldn't find much. The killers associated with The Society were well-trained and employed illegal charms bought on the black market to shield their deeds. None of the neighbors saw or heard a thing, even though the family must have screamed in agony through their ordeal.

Once the RIU was done, members from the Fae Guild would come to test for charms and spells. They always found the remnant of a spell, usually one that would allow the killers to get away, and perhaps more importantly, one that was designed to degrade over time, so that the bodies would be found.

But what good did that do? The Guild could identify a charm, but they couldn't prevent another one from being created. And the black market was alive and well in his realm.

The woman who'd been cleansing his uniform completed her task. She rose and patted Malik's shoulder. "The Goddess's blessings on you, Mastyr." She then moved slowly down the steps, weeping anew.

One of his lieutenants, Evan, flew in, his expression somber. "Came as fast as I could from the north. We found three Invictus pairs. Took care of them."

"Three?" Malik's realm had the fewest Invictus incursions of any of the Nine Realms. That there had been three sounded an alarm inside his head.

"Yes." Evan nodded. "I thought it strange as well."

The last thing Malik needed was a sudden arrival of wraith-pairs into his realm. He had enough problems with The Society hunting down and murdering innocent citizens.

Evan dipped his chin in the direction of the front door. "How bad is it?"

For a few seconds, Malik numbed out again as the images once more flowed through his mind. He couldn't speak.

"Malik?"

He shifted his gaze to Evan. "It's never been worse. Two little boys. A family of four elves. Don't go in there. They were tortured. Forensics is doing its thing anyway."

Evan had young children. As though struck at the back of his knees, Evan dropped suddenly to sit on the porch, his long Guardsman legs angling down three steps. "Shit." He covered his face with his hand.

The door slammed open and the RIU agent stalked out of the house, his face ashen. He didn't respond when Malik called to him. The tall fae, renowned for his ability to track serial predators, walked up High Street, refusing to answer questions thrust at him by the village inhabitants. He disappeared around the bend, not looking back.

Malik understood. But the sight of one of his toughest agents coming apart just as Malik had, shifted something inside him. Something had to give. He'd been putting off a critical decision for a long time now, hating what needed to be done. But this execution had ended the debate.

A troll, driving a horse-drawn cart, drew close to the porch. "That cursed family had wraith-blood and got what they deserved." He spat and plied his whip again.

Some cheered the troll's harsh words, while others booed and shouted protests against half-breed hate-speech.

And this was what caused Malik the most despair — that his realm was divided. A large number of his people hated wraiths with a passion because of the Invictus, while others believed that innocent wraiths, unaffected by Margetta the Ancient Fae, should be tolerated and accepted like any other realm-person. It was Margetta who turned wraiths into a killing force.

But as the troll and his cart disappeared down a side lane that led into the forest, Malik knew the time had come to make a significant change, and one he'd hoped to avoid. He would get the Sidhe Council to agree to a mandate, commanding the removal of every last half-breed to Swanicott Realm for all of Ashleaf. Swanicott had one of the few protected wraith colonies in the entire Nine Realms and the mastyr there had offered Malik the opportunity countless times to take in his endangered half-breeds.

The death of the twin elven boys had finally finished off his last resistance to relocation as a solution to the divide in his realm.

He basically had a terrorist organization working inside his realm, and he didn't have the ability to uncover the principal organizers and bring them to justice. He'd never believed in relocation as a solution, nor did his vast number of supporters. But unless he saved the several thousand realm-folk who carried wraith-blood in their veins, he would face decades of exactly this kind of murder.

And there was one other issue that needed to be addressed.

Willow.

He thought about what he'd done just before dawn and how he'd let himself get distracted with his longings for Willow. Maybe if he hadn't let his guard down and finished up his nightly patrols with a visit to her favorite pool, maybe something would have alerted him to the terrible events here in Birchingwood.

Maybe he'd been distracted, maybe not. But if there was the smallest chance his pursuit of Willow had interfered with his proper managing of Ashleaf, then he needed to find some way to end his obsession.

And just as these thoughts passed through his mind, suddenly, he felt Willow's presence. In response, his heart started pounding hard in his chest.

Scanning the crowds clumped all along High Street, he finally caught sight of her at the edge of the forest. She had a soft glow around her that meant she'd covered herself in a fae charm, just as she did when she went shopping in the various villages.

And as had happened the first time he saw her at market day in Cherry Hollow, and every time he'd seen her since, he felt stunned by the sight of her. She wore a pair of jeans and a tank top against the warm September day, and her red wavy hair hung free about her shoulders.

She was so beautiful that something inside his brain started sending flashes of lightning that traveled to every part of his body. Some realm part of him *knew* her, *recognized her* as more than just a woman he wanted to take to bed. Was Miriam right? Did he need to take a serious look at what was really happening between himself and Willow?

He forced himself to take a breath, then another.

He started to contact her telepathically, when he felt her rapping against his mind. Again, the woman was powerful.

He allowed the communication. *Hello, Willow.*

Malik, we need to fix this. I need you to stop coming after me. I have important duties that your presence interferes with, and I can't allow this to go on.

He was surprised, which reminded him that he really knew very little about this woman. But what duties was she referring to? He knew she was focused on something, but on what? And why did she live such a secretive life?

Still holding her gaze, he responded, *I feel the same way.*

He dropped down to the top step and put a hand on Evan's shoulder. "I have something I have to take care of right now. Let me know how the investigation goes. I'm hoping like hell we'll learn something, but I'm not holding my breath."

Evan looked up at him, then gained his feet. "I'll look after things here." He pressed the heels of his palms to wet eyes.

That's what he loved about the Guardsmen, whether they were his Vampire Guard or Troll Brigade. They were good, honest men, with great hearts, and he experienced a camaraderie with them that equaled nothing else in his life.

"Call me if you need me."

He shifted to levitated flight and sped slowly along the cobbled street in Willow's direction. He wasn't surprised that before he reached her, she turned and moved up the path, though not running this time so that he'd be able to follow her.

He thought he understood. If he paused at the edge of the village to talk to her, it would look as though he was speaking to himself. Few in Ashleaf Realm would have the power to see through Willow's fae-charm glow.

~ ~ ~

Willow felt Malik behind her, moving at a steady clip. She wanted to be well away from the village before she engaged in conversation with him. It also gave her time to deal with the oppressive weight that the deaths of the elven family had created in her heart.

She pathed, *I'll be heading back to my gate. We can speak there without being observed.*

Thought as much, and yes, it's a good idea.

She didn't try to converse more. What she needed to say, needed to *show* him, wouldn't be served well through a mere exchange of words. And Malik still needed some time to recover from what he'd witnessed. She did as well, because the vision kept rolling through her mind of seeing him inside the elven home.

Covering the thirty miles fairly slowly gave her much needed distance from Birchingwood, both emotionally and physically. By the time she held open the wrought iron gate that led onto her land, she could sense that like her, Malik's grief had lessened.

"I can feel the protective charm," Malik said as she closed the tall gate behind him.

"I was taught by the best and you know her well. Alexandra the Bad."

"I do."

Most realm-folk wouldn't be able to cross this boundary, either on foot by opening the gate or by flying above it. She had powerful charms in place that should have kept even Axton off her lands, which was another sign that a fae of exceptional ability was helping him.

She glanced at Malik. "And you are one of the few who can overcome the charm."

At that, he smiled, and her breath caught all over again. For a moment Willow felt as though the wind had been knocked out of her. She wanted to say something, but her mind got all tangled up in being so close to Malik at long last.

Until this moment, she'd looked at him either at a distance or through the veil of the vines. Now here he was, flesh and blood, a slight sheen of sweat on his forehead, but offering no other sign that flying for thirty miles had cost him much energy.

But it was his deep brown eyes cut with so much sadness that held her captive. She could feel all that he'd experienced in the elven cobbler's house. "Malik, I'm so sorry."

He looked confused for a moment. "For running from me?"

She shook her head. "For what happened in Birchingwood."

He nodded slowly. "It will take some time before I'll be able to let those images go. We've had too many deaths." She felt his thoughts fall inward and for that reason she remained silent.

Her heart thrummed heavily in response, his grief making her wish there was something she could do to help. But she was feeling too much for Malik on every possible level — her desire for him, her admiration, her compassion, her understanding of what he suffered as ruler of Ashleaf. "There were children in that house, weren't there?"

"Yes, twin boys." He turned away to settle his gaze on the dense forest surrounding the path. "But I intend for this murder to be the last in my realm."

She could feel that he'd come to a decision, but even through the level of his determination, once more a familiar sadness came through.

"And I hope very much that it is." She glanced up the path, in the direction of the colony. "And now there's something I need to show you."

She moved on, walking swiftly along a path as familiar as the rocks in the stream below her treehouse. He followed behind her, since the route was narrow. She listened to the birds, to the hollow sounds as she crossed a wooden bridge over yet another stream, and to the sounds of Malik's heavier footfalls behind her.

When the path split, she paused, turning to him. "Do you know where we are?"

He gestured with a toss of his arm to the path on the right that led northeast. "That will take you to your treehouse complex, but I have to admit I don't know where this western path goes, and I thought I knew every footpath in Ashleaf."

Throughout her initial trip to Birchingwood, she'd debated just how much to tell him about the wraith colony. In the end, she'd decided to keep her revelations, at least for now, down to a minimum.

Heading west, she spoke to him over her shoulder. "You'll be seeing more of the same vines soon, like the ones at my gate, my waterfall, and around the base of the oaks at my treehouse complex."

"It's an unusual vine, isn't it?"

"Very."

"I'm curious, though, why it hasn't overtaken the surrounding forest like most vines would?"

"I keep it in check," was all she was willing to say.

The distance to the colony from the fork in the path wasn't far, maybe half-a-mile to the granite monolith and the vines that shrouded the entrance. Because she needed him to see why he had never been able to find her when he'd given chase, she put on a sudden burst of speed intending to vanish into the vines, then show herself to him.

She heard him shout his protest as she flew over a waterfall and sped the remaining quarter mile to the monolith. "You'll see soon enough," she called back.

Once there, she melted into the vines that guarded the entrance to the wraith-colony. She held two of her favorite thick stems and watched his arrival as he topped the last rise of land, his Guardsman coat flapping behind him. He was one pissed off vampire, which was something that made her smile.

"Willow? What the fuck?"

Malik was all Guardsman and though she rarely cursed herself, she knew that fighting men needed many avenues to let off steam, profanity being one of them.

"Okay, now I'm pissed. Why did you bring me all this way if just to make me chase you again? What kind of game are you playing?"

She saw him through the haze of her protective vine charm and suddenly felt very sad. After this night, she would probably never see him again, and for that reason she took a moment to just look at him, at his brown eyes and strong cheekbones, and at his long, thick, dark brown hair, which had a slight wave and was caught in the traditional Guardsman clasp. How many times had she imagined sinking her hands into his hair?

She was a hopeless case where Malik was concerned. He'd played a prominent role in her fantasies for so long and now she was going to expose one of her secrets to him, something only he would know. And after which, she would send him away forever.

"Willow, please don't do this." He turned in a full circle, looking for her.

She touched his mind telepathically. *I didn't bring you here to torment you, Mastyr, but rather to show you something. Please, turn toward the vines.*

He shifted in her direction, his brow furrowed. He looked deeply distressed, which helped her to know just how frustrating all the chases had been for him.

Slowly, she willed the vines to part for her, then removed the protective spell. His eyes widened as she stepped from the vines.

He stared at her for a long time, before saying, "You have more power than even Alexandra, don't you? So why aren't you head of the Fae Guild?"

It seemed so much like Malik that he would address these issues first and not that she'd been hiding herself in the vines at the end of every chase.

She drew in a deep breath, suddenly nervous that she was about to reveal other things about herself, things she'd taken a vow never to reveal. Yet she trusted Malik, and he needed to know why he had to leave her alone from this moment forward. "There's a simple reason; I have the ability to create a protective shield."

He blinked, then asked, "But what are you protecting?"

Now for the white lie. She stepped back and gestured to the beautiful hanging vines. "For decades now, I've guarded several wraith families who live on my land behind these vines. Pure blooded wraiths."

He met her gaze, searching her eyes. "Holy shit. And you're absolutely serious."

His words surprised her. "Of course I am. Why wouldn't I be? Why would I say something like that and not mean it?"

He turned toward the vines. "How many families?"

"A few."

"Where did they come from?"

"They were always on this land."

He drew close to the vines and touched them. "I can feel your frequency where my fingers connect." He continued to touch and pat the vines at various intervals. "And the entrance is somewhere nearby, isn't it?"

She released a heavy sigh. "Yes, but please don't ask me to take you inside. I've taken a vow to keep their presence in your realm a secret."

He shook his head. "You said these are full-blooded wraiths?"

She nodded.

"Shit." She felt his despair all over again as he added quietly, "No wraith is safe in Ashleaf."

"And that's why they stay hidden behind my shield."

He turned toward her, his frown deepening, his expression full of concern. "Is this why I always feel that you're focused on something else whenever I'm around you?"

She nodded, grateful that he was finally coming to understand. "Yes. I'm constantly streaming energy to the shield." She almost told him about Axton's recent attempt to breach the entrance, but was afraid of revealing too much. Besides, if she stayed on alert, she felt certain she could deal with Axton herself. "Mastyr, I can't be distracted and this is why I've brought you here. It takes tremendous concentration to sustain the shield." She didn't go into how this had worsened in recent years. "Do you understand?"

"I'm familiar with the feeling."

"I know you are. We're alike in that way."

He nodded, but his frown had deepened. "Critical duties to fulfill."

She felt grateful that he'd understood her so readily.

"Willow, I think you should know that I've come to a decision to begin the relocation process. You're aware of the controversy?"

"Of course, and I'm staunchly opposed. Why let Axton and his kind win?"

He pressed his lips together. "Because I won't have another death on my hands. Not one more. Not after witnessing the Birchingwood murders." He waved a hand to encompass the vines. "And I think these families should be part of that relocation."

She shook her head. "No. You mustn't attempt to remove them." Her gaze dropped to the ground. She felt the heart of the Nine Realms beneath her feet, a soft frequency that also protested his decision. Lifting her gaze back to him, she added, "The wraiths must stay here. I believe there have always been wraiths in Ashleaf and that they serve a purpose here."

"Children died, Willow. Babies, really."

She drew close and put her hand on his shoulder, letting waves of compassion flow. He turned toward her, eyes wide once more. "Sweet Goddess," he murmured. "You have so much power."

As she stared into his eyes, the affection and admiration she felt for him rose once more. He was such a worthy man and maybe because she'd made physical contact, she couldn't seem to suppress the desire that swept through her. What went through her mind as her body heated up yet again, was that more than anything in the world she wanted to ask him to come home with her.

And it would involve a lot more than just talking things through.

She opened her mouth to speak and tell him he should leave now and to forget about relocating any of the wraiths and half-breeds in his realm. Instead, other words tumbled out, "Would you like to come home with me, just once? To be with me?"

~ ~ ~

Malik felt Willow's mating frequency flowing over him in heavy, needful waves. The invitation was clear. And as he stared into her beautiful, hazel eyes, he knew what his answer would be. "Yes, I'd love to be with you."

For the first time ever he'd be inside her house.

The metaphor wasn't lost on him, and desire surged all over again. What was it about Willow that had him mad with need?

Without her knowing, he'd made more than one circuit around her treehouse dwelling, but he'd respected her privacy, refusing to cross the threshold when she wasn't there. He would never do that.

But now he had an invitation.

She put two fingers to her lips, and her eyes widened.

"What is it?" He stepped toward her, closing an already small gap.

"It's, I don't know. The way you smell. You have this lush forest scent, like the streams and the rocks, and the fragrance of the trees and the leaves — everything."

Her lips parted and her eyes closed as she drew a very deep breath.

What returned to him was an answering scent, so full of rain-in-the-forest and sex that his knees almost buckled. He couldn't prevent the groan that escaped his throat.

This was not exactly how he'd imagined this meeting would go. He'd intended to finish this insanity between them. Instead, she'd invited him back to her house and apparently he intended to go with her. "Won't you be distracted?"

Oddly, she looked down at her feet again. "I feel certain that it will be all right. In fact, I know it will, which makes no sense. But my power is flowing better than ever right now. The col—that is, the families will be fine."

Malik was grateful for his Guard coat because right now it covered a multitude of sins. But he stood tottering on the fence. He should break with Willow. He should leave her land and never look back. She would be better off and so would he.

Yet he couldn't make his feet move.

What he'd desired for two years was right here in front of him with an invitation.

"Malik?"

He even loved her voice, a delicate melodious sound that wrenched his heart.

But when she placed her hand on his shoulder again, as though to gentle him down, things went completely haywire. He'd been holding back for two years and now here she was touching him.

Without thinking, he dragged her into his arms, slanting his lips over hers, all but bending his massive Guardsman body over hers.

She cried out, and he should have stopped. But the cry caused her lips to part, and he slid his tongue inside, moaning his need, his desire, the depth of his longing for her.

He kissed her as though this was the first kiss man had ever given woman. He plunged his tongue in and out, savoring the warm wet nest that made him hunger for what resided between her legs.

He was so lost in the experience, of finally being able to take her in his arms, that only after a full minute did he come to an awareness that she was into this as much as he was.

Her hands had dislodged his Guardsman clasp, and she'd sunk her fingers into his hair. At the same time, she made odd warbling sounds like an Ashleaf night-bird.

The knowledge that she wanted him as desperately as he craved her and was savoring the kiss as much as he was, encouraged him. *Willow, I've longed for you, for this, to be close to you. Tell me it's been the same with you.*

You know it has, Malik. But I've been without companionship for so long, though, that I fear what I'm feeling is more about repressed need than about you.

He didn't care the source, only that she wanted him with a passion that matched his own.

He slid his hand down to her buttocks, pressing her against what was so hard and ready for her. She whimpered, then drew back. Her lips were swollen as she clung to him. "I want you to see my home. Do you want to come with?"

He nodded, knowing he'd just fallen into the *hopeless* category.

As she drew away from him, the light forest-rain scent of her sex flooded the space between. He could tell she was about to turn away from him in order to begin the trek, but he caught her up in his arms, cradling her. "I know the way. Let me fly you."

She put her arms around his neck. "I would love that."

Even though this vine-covered monolith was new to him, his destination was as familiar as the night sky above. Using his vampire homing senses, he quickly laid out the best route.

As he levitated, Malik began to feel just how much of Willow's land held her fae magic, as though she'd somehow connected with the earth itself. Miriam's words came back to him about exploring the realm-ness that seemed to be in constant motion between himself and Willow.

He could have flown her up above the forest canopy, but he didn't want to. Willow was the forest and everything wild that grew and thrived on her land.

He flew slowly at first, then more quickly, taking care not to let any wayward branches slap at Willow or cut her arms or legs. His chest swelled at having her so close, this woman who shielded several wraith families.

Now that he understood her focus, he appreciated her all the more. But he wondered why she'd kept this a secret from him? Surely, she understood that he damn well knew the difference between the Invictus wraith-pairs and those innocent wraiths who had lived in the Nine Realms from the beginning?

Maybe in time, she would tell him. She'd spoken of a vow, but why had it been necessary?

As he turned his attention to her more and more, he started to feel the layers of her. His desire had so dominated his male drive that only now, as he flew toward the ridge where her treehouse had been built, could he feel the enormous responsibility she carried in protecting these wraiths.

He slowed as the trail in the oak wood opened up and her primary residence came into view. She'd built her home on the side of a small ravine, as many of the Ashleaf inhabitants did. Open pasture land was rare in his realm and most of it commandeered for the raising of goats and sheep. More than once, he'd tried to talk to her while she was at her house, but she took off from there and he gave chase. And if he had to give chase, he preferred meeting her first at the pool, bastard that he was.

The first of her five treehouses that made up her complex looked completely deceiving, since it was on the level of the path. But he knew the land dropped away sharply, at least thirty feet to the stream and small waterfall below.

But the curved walkway with a protective wood railing and a cut-out diamond on every other oiled panel, had a charm familiar to the mountain forests of Ashleaf.

As he set her on her feet, he could feel that the protective spell was stronger this close to her house.

She glanced up at him, her hazel eyes glittering as she took his hand. "I'm glad you're here, Malik. I've wanted to speak with you, to be with you for such a long time."

"And I've wanted to be here." He then made his confession about having spent time on this part of her property.

"But you never went inside?" Her brows rose, but she didn't seem upset.

"Of course not."

At that, she smiled. "I wouldn't have minded. Anyone else, probably, but not you. I trust you because I've watched how you govern your realm and I knew of the laws you instituted when you took Axton's place."

"That's kind of you to say so, but until I rid Ashleaf of The Society, I'll never be at peace."

"One day you will. I'm confident of that."

He stared into her hazel eyes, wondering yet again what this was between them.

He moved to the railing near the front door and looked down. The entire hillside had been planted and grown lush with ferns. Below, a mature vegetable plot in stone supported terraces, ranged in the direction of the stream. "You haul the water?"

She chuckled. "No. Do you see the far tree and the pipe? I have a small electric pump."

Solar power had made a lot of things possible in his realm in the past few years.

"It's very peaceful here."

She stood beside him, also looking down at her garden and the stream, as well as a small waterfall twenty or so yards to the north. Ashleaf had thousands of similar waterfalls.

"I've worked hard to make my home a haven. It's been necessary because of the work I do on behalf of the wraiths."

He turned toward her. "I can only imagine, and I'm amazed that you've sacrificed so much to help them."

At that, she smiled again. She had beautiful even teeth. "Well, I don't do anything that you're not doing, Mastyr."

He shook his head. "Please call me Malik. Like you did before."

But she placed a quick hand on his arm. "It's my way of telling you how much I respect what you've done as Mastyr of Ashleaf. You inspire me."

"I do?" He was surprised. He just didn't think of himself in those terms.

"Of course. Your dedication of service keeps me committed to protecting my wraiths."

The air between them shifted once more, especially since she still had her hand on his arm. Desire for her raged all over again, and he was stunned how quickly even just a touch or a word of praise could make him want her so much.

A blush covered her cheeks, and her fresh forest-rain scent rose in the air. "Why don't you come inside?"

Maybe it was her choice of words, but he almost attacked her again.

Instead, he restrained himself, and as she headed toward the door, he quickly moved around her, pulling the door open so that she could go in before him.

This part of her treehouse complex housed her living room, kitchen, and dining room. Two separate doors led to different rope bridges, one leading up into the oak canopy, the other to a lower level.

She gestured to the one leading up. "My bedroom and bathroom are up there. I saved the highest space for sleeping. The lower level is for meditation and has a porch where I spend a lot of my time. I often have tea out there. Sometimes a beer or two.

"I like that."

She smiled. "Then off the kitchen, is a third door that leads to my lower workrooms, one for storage and canning and the last for my gardening equipment and anything else pertaining to the function of my home."

Malik approved of the overall craftsmanship. "You had some excellent workers on this project."

"The best trolls. Every finish is superb." A smooth, stained branch ran from floor-to-ceiling, supporting the kitchen island.

She'd built the house on larger lines than most, so even his Guardsman body felt comfortable in the space.

He felt something new coming from her however, and turned once more in her direction. She leaned against the supporting branch, her hands behind her and he caught her looking him up and down.

Then he saw something that both startled him yet made his leathers tight across the zipper. Small white fangs appeared and were now pressing onto her lower lip. Fangs smaller than a vampire's.

He knew what they were at once: Wraith fangs.

"Willow?"

She lifted her gaze. Her hazel eyes were dark, her pupils dilated. "Yes?" Because of her fangs, she had a slight lisp.

She covered them quickly with her fingers and her cheeks flamed a dark peach color.

He went to her and took her hand away, so that he could see the sharp points again. Very carefully, he thumbed her lips and rubbed the edges of the fangs. "I don't think I've seen anything more beautiful than these."

"I didn't mean to … it's just that …"

"I know." The time had come. "Why don't you show me your bedroom, and I'll happily let you tap in anywhere you want to." Bold words.

In response, she almost fell, but he slid his arm around her waist, supporting her. "Knees buckled?"

"Uh-huh. It's been a long time. Way too long. But please know nothing permanent can come of this."

"I know, and I'm with you. We both need to stay focused on our separate duties. But right now, I'm going to focus on you."

She whimpered softly, leaning her head against his shoulder.

He picked her up and flew her slowly out the door toward her bedroom. The fresh smell of the oak wood spilled over him.

When he crossed the solid wood bridge and reached the open doorway to her treehouse bedroom, he paused on the threshold. He didn't usually attach a lot of meaning to sex, or even to where a woman slept. But something about this moment felt sacred. Once more he experienced the vibrations from deep in the earth as though Willow and now he had a connection to the land.

Miriam had been right; everything about his relationship with Willow felt very realm.

The room had windows on each side. And just like that, vines suddenly appeared at the long, open window above the bed. He had no doubt he was looking at Willow's magic, and that the vines that grew at the base of the central oak, had just climbed into her room.

She moved in his arms and he set her down.

"Your vines are here."

She glanced back at the bed. "Yes, they are, but don't worry; they're part of me."

"I'm not worried, Willow, not on any level. You spoke of trusting me, but I feel the same way about you."

She turned back to him and caught his face in her hands, kissing him once on the lips. "Will you let me do something for you? It would mean a lot to me, a sort of ritual."

He'd known many fae through the years and knew that they placed great value on the order of things. "I'd be honored."

She drew a deep breath and he felt how nervous she was. But what she said surprised him. "Take off your clothes."

~ ~ ~

Willow felt her cheeks grow warm, having just told the Mastyr of Ashleaf to essentially get naked. She added quickly, "I'll be right back."

She moved into the small adjacent bathroom and filled a white ceramic basin with cool water. Afterward, she removed her clothes then donned her thin, white, floor-length robe. She took a moment to brush out her long hair.

She heard Malik cursing. Right afterward, the sound of his boots striking the wood floor reverberated into the bathroom. The Guardsmen wore thigh boots over leathers, a very masculine, sexy look, but they couldn't always be easy to remove.

Carrying the basin and two soft cloths, she stopped on the threshold. He'd laid out his clothes on a ladder-back woven chair by the window opposite the bed.

And he was naked.

She couldn't believe that after two years of painful longing he was finally here. Given her level of responsibility, she might only get to experience this with him once, but she wanted to do it right. Besides, the earth sustained her as though approving of what she was doing, and she knew the colony was safe.

Bidding him stand on the oval rag-rug that she'd made herself, she dipped the cloth in the water. She sank to her knees and began with his feet and cleansed him, her heart very full, her fangs sitting on her lower lip because she was terribly aroused. She washed his legs and felt his hand on her head in soft, affectionate strokes.

His very tender touch was just as she'd imagined. She sensed his emotions as well that he was somewhat in awe of what she was doing. At the same time, his mating vibration came to life, a soft hum in the center of his being, which naturally stirred her own needs.

Was this the man for her, the mastyr of an entire realm?

Her pleasure was intense as she asked him to spread his legs. She carefully worked the cool, damp cloth over his testicles and cock, the latter of which was thick and long and quite perfect.

And fully erect.

She kissed his groin on either side, just above the veins. She could smell his blood because of her latent wraith abilities. Looking up at him, she said, "Your blood smells of the richest part of the forest, Malik. Just like you."

"And yours smells like the forest after a rain. That clean, almost spiritual fragrance."

She smiled. "I like that you've said it that way."

She busied herself again, cleansing his abdomen and chest, taking her time, wiping down both arms. She tended to his back and his buttocks in the same way.

When she was done, she took the basin back into the bathroom and returned with her brush. Pulling back the sheets, she had him sit on the side of the bed and took her time brushing out his Guardsman hair.

As Willow ran her hands down his hair, she could feel the subtle vibration. "Your hair makes you stronger."

"That is our belief."

"I can feel the frequency." She rose as she spoke, and while standing in front of him, she removed her white robe.

His eyes flared, but he made no move to touch her. Instead, he waited, letting her lead the moment.

Her heart beat hard now, ready to be touched and loved by Malik after so many months of painful longing. Without saying anything, she stretched out on her stomach on the bed and waited.

Closing her eyes, she expected Malik to join her. Instead, the floor creaked and a moment later, she heard the water running. She lifted up on her forearms and tears came to her eyes when he returned with the basin.

He took his time as well, beginning with her feet and washed her head-to-foot. Tears began to fall and she couldn't seem to stop them. She'd bathed Malik because she revered what he did for her kind. But to have him return what was for her a very sacred act, struck her deep in her soul.

When she turned over and he cleansed her legs, then deep between her thighs, desire began to rise once more, the way it had for the past two years.

He swept the cloth upward and over her abdomen, the sensation leaving a trail of shivers. Her breasts puckered and he leaned down and half-sucked, half-kissed each in turn.

She cupped his face in her hand and turned him toward her. This was Malik, the man who had chased her, whom she'd spurned. Now he was here.

Her heart labored in her chest as though anxious to feed him. She wanted him to bite her and she wanted to use her fangs. Something she'd never done before. But Malik's blood called to her.

He set the cloth and the basin aside and kissed her, moving between her legs. "Your fangs are beautiful."

Her tongue emerged between them and he groaned, his forest scent permeating the air.

The next moment, in response to her growing need, the vines at the open window began to move down the white, cast iron frame behind her.

He lifted up, his eyes widening. "The vines are moving now."

She slid her hands over his shoulders. "They're responding to me. They'll be part of what we'll do together, if that's all right with you?"

He glanced down as one of the vines touched his arm and slid over him, caressing him. He closed his eyes. "Sweet Goddess, that feels good and no, I don't mind, because this feels like you. But what exactly are you doing?"

"Needing you to make love to me, that's all. I'm connected to the vines on my land. I can't explain it. They hide me and they protect the wraith families. They respond to my thoughts and desires, and they would even protect me at my command."

Another vine now moved across his back and he moaned. "I've never experienced anything like this."

"Is it too strange, Malik? If I concentrate, I can make them leave."

"No," he answered quickly. "I want them to stay."

She smiled, because she could feel how much he was enjoying the sensation. "You probably should be inside me."

He gave her an answering smile. "I could come so easily right now."

"I know. Me, too." She shifted her hips, letting him know that she needed him filling her. The foreplay had lasted two years and she was ready.

The moment she felt his cock at her entrance, a heavy moan left her throat. The physical connection soared through her, a vibration all its own, and small cries left her mouth at the exquisite feel of what was so hard and began moving inside her.

He pushed, and her whole body writhed. The vines stroked her hair and her face and she watched one slide across his neck, where she wanted her hand to be. When she moved her hand, the vine gave way and covered hers adding the smallest pressure so that she caressed Malik with the vine aiding her.

Inelegant yet erotic guttural sounds left his throat. "Never been like this … the vines."

"I know. This is new to me as well."

"It is?"

She met his gaze. "Yes. All new. Oh, Malik."

Passion rose to a dizzying height as he kissed her hard. Because of the vines, she could feel what they felt like to him, as though the realm itself, which he loved with all his heart, was caressing him. What a strange mystery this had become, this sharing with Malik, full of the heights and depths of all of life experience. She'd never felt more connected to the earth on which she lived, to the frequencies beating deep in her land, to the vines that helped her to protect the colony.

His tongue penetrated her mouth, and moved in rhythm to his thrusts between her legs. Several vines slid beneath her and she felt them wrapping tenderly around Malik as well.

He continued to kiss her, their bodies moving in such an exquisite motion and in sync with her heart.

He drew back slightly and presented his wrist. "Take my blood, Willow. I offer it for the way you've laid down your life to protect the innocent."

She lifted her hand and the vines gave way just enough to allow for her movements. She pressed his wrist to her small fangs and with the memories given to her by all the wraiths in her maternal family line, she struck quickly, then began to suck.

The first hit of his blood caused her to clench deep and in response, Malik groaned.

She held his gaze as the erotic flavor of his blood poured over her tongue. Power moved through her and the vines tightened and released in response. Everything was so sensual and erotic that she could hardly control herself.

When she began pulling on him low, deep in her well, she forced herself to stop or he would come. They both would. And she knew exactly how and when she wanted to reach the pinnacle. She wanted to be with him in that moment, his fangs having opened her vein, his mouth sucking down what she could feel he needed more than anything else right now.

She breathed hard, trying to calm down.

He'd squeezed his eyes shut, doing the same thing.

Only how to hold on, to make the moment last?

Chapter Three

Malik had imagined being in bed with Willow for a long time now. But even the best of fantasies hadn't come close to this erotic reality. He felt lost in her arms, barely able to make two thoughts connect.

The vines.

Sweet Goddess, the vines alone had his balls ready to release. The tendrils held him tight to Willow, and moved as he moved. Yet he could feel that with the slightest resistance the vines would shift and give way.

And Willow's fangs. The piercing had sent a thrill straight through his cock and he'd almost come … again. He was so ready to let go that every muscle in his body twitched with anticipation.

He could feel that she was close as well, each of them riding the edge.

She looked so beautiful suckling at his wrist, her eyes glittering. He wanted her neck. His stomach, always cramping, now screamed for what he'd been desiring for the past two years.

She suddenly released his wrist. "Malik, now, please. I'm right there. Right there." She squeezed her eyes shut.

"Me, too."

Rolling her head, she swept her auburn hair away from her neck. The vines adjusted for each movement. "Please, do it. Take from me. I need to feed you. So heavy in my chest. And I'm ready to release. So close."

He was too lost to make sense of all her words, but he got her meaning, especially when his eyes zeroed in on the vein beating in her throat.

He leaned close, his hips still working her low, and licked a line up her neck. Usually this would encourage the vein to rise, but hers was already pulsing and waiting.

His fangs descended and in a swift strike, he broke through. Her blood flowed into his mouth.

The world disappeared as the flavor of her life-force hit his tongue, his throat, then traveled like exquisite liquid fire into his stomach. Fireworks exploded within, sending her power into his blood-stream. The muscles of his arms flexed and released. His buttocks as well. He felt stronger, suddenly, as he moved his hips faster.

His mind spun as he continued to drink, taking the fire down his throat.

Willow whimpered and writhed beneath him. She took shallow breaths, holding herself on the cliff.

He felt something real and thrilling move through him. He couldn't wait any longer and let go of her neck. He lifted up on his forearms so that he could look down at her, the vines giving way to his movements, then wrapping around him once more. Her eyes were closed, her body in a state of passionate suspension.

"Look at me, Willow."

Her eyes opened slowly.

He smiled and increased his speed. "Come with me. Now."

She nodded. "Yes."

At the same time, he sent a vibration through his cock, one that had his balls seizing and her well pulling on him. She cried out and the vines began moving at the same time in quick small jerks so that he was shouting as well.

Lightning streaks of pleasure flowed through his cock as ecstasy arrived. Willow's cries of release and pleasure added to the incredible mix of sensations that wouldn't stop. The forest scent of her sex filled his nostrils, adding one more layer.

The orgasm kept coming as he filled her full of all that he was as a man.

Her nails dug into his shoulders as she continued to cry out.

When she finally eased down, he would have stopped, but his cock was still hard and he felt the impossible happen. "Willow? Can you come a second time?"

Her eyes opened wide. "Really?"

"Oh, yeah. It must be your blood."

"And yours, because I'm still feeling you and loving your cock. Malik." Her eyes rolled and her body once more tensed. "I'm ready."

He sped up again, moving fast like only a vampire could move.

This time Willow screamed and the vines vibrated against his skin, stroking him between his legs. When he came this time, he shouted repeatedly. He felt as one let loose like a great northern wind, his body releasing as it never had before.

When at last his shouts dimmed and Willow's cries became soft moans, he felt the sweet tightness of her well with his last thrust. He stayed within as he relaxed against her, and the vines began to loosen their grip, receding slowly.

Even that sensation soothed him in a way he just didn't understand. Some kind of miracle had come to him with Willow, though he couldn't quite make sense of it. She was incredibly powerful and connected to these vines with a fae magic he'd never heard of before.

Yet the vines reflected the sweetness of her disposition. There was nothing of war in Willow, only of love, kindness and protection.

As he rested on her body, he savored the mounds of her breasts against his chest, the way she stroked the nape of his neck, and that she played with his long hair.

Her breathing evened out, and in time his did as well.

He was so replete; he could hardly move. He hadn't felt this way in a long time, if ever, as though he'd come home after being away for centuries.

Was Willow *his home*?

Even if she was, other memories intruded of how her father had died and that Malik was responsible for his death, of his need to stay focused on his realm, and of his deep commitment to prevent The Society from hurting Ashleaf one more time.

Slowly, the feel-good of the moment faded and his responsibilities returned. He should call Evan and see how things were going. "I have to get back to my men."

She rubbed both of his shoulders. "I know. And I need to shift my focus to the wraith … that is, to those families I'm protecting."

He eased out of her and went into the bathroom. He found a cloth in a woven basket below the sink and brought it back to Willow. He tucked it between her legs, smiling down at her. "Thought you might need this."

She smiled softly, her gaze full of affection. "Thank you. For everything, Malik. This was extraordinary. I can't tell you how much this meant to me. I feel now as though I could continue another century because I swear your blood has given me some much-needed strength."

At first her words pleased him, then suddenly they spoke to his own condition. Putting a hand to his stomach, a terrible suspicion ripped through his mind.

She leaned up on her elbows as the last of the vines slipped back through the window. "What is it?"

"I'm not sure." The suspicion worked in him badly, disrupting his peace. But he didn't want to speak the words out loud. "I just feel a need to be going."

She reached out and grabbed his arm. "Then do that, Malik, but without any guilt. And please, don't set anything aside for me or worry about offending me. Please. This is very important to me."

Her words stunned him. He'd had a few, brief relationships over the decades and usually the opposite words fell from a woman's lips, always demanding more not less. He knew then that whatever this was between them would never be simple.

He nodded. "I have to go." But panic had started eating up his heart. He touched his stomach and cringed once more. This couldn't be happening.

He went into the bathroom and cleaned up, then returned to don his clothes. Once he was dressed and ready to get the hell out of there, Willow caught his arms and kissed him once on the lips, a full kiss.

"Malik, I can feel your distress. But truly, you don't have to think of me ever again. This finishes things. We're agreed on that, right?"

"Absolutely." Her words sort of eased him. Somehow he'd make this right, despite what he'd begun to believe was the horrible truth about who she really was in his life.

He moved unsteadily to the doorway and once on the bridge, he drew in a deep breath, willing the truth away.

He flew, but almost crashed straight into a thick branch of oak that would have had no give. Talk about distracted.

He'd meant to go south, to return to his Guard facility. Instead, his mind was so muddled with this latest bizarre turn of events that he flew north.

What he believed might be true felt almost tragic to him. He had nothing to give Willow and he'd been the cause of her father's death.

But he kept going north because he had to think.

As he flew, he used his cell to let Evan know where he was and that he'd be back in about half an hour. Evan related that things in Birchingwood had calmed down considerably and that most of the villagers had started going about their business. The RIU agent had finally returned to complete his investigation. "Otherwise, the realm is quiet. No Invictus sightings tonight."

"Good. That's good." He took a deep breath. "I'll talk to you later."

When he reached his destination, he landed on a massive slab of granite that protruded from the hilltop of one of Ashleaf's highest mountain ridges over a mile high.

He placed a hand on his stomach once more and shook his head slowly in complete disbelief. He wanted to deny that the lack of cramping he experienced meant something, but he felt it in his bones that Willow's blood had strengthened him. Even his muscles felt bulked up. He looked down at his thighs and could see that his leathers were tighter than before.

Power flowed through him as well with streams of energy that made him feel like he could do anything.

But it couldn't be true.

Please don't let it be true.

His mind rolled backward to how Willow had bathed him. And that's when a profound longing slammed through him all over again, and he stumbled, losing his footing.

He levitated quickly or he would have fallen over the precipice.

Sweet Goddess, this just could not be happening. Not to him.

And the sex and the vines and Willow's soft yielding body beneath his ... and her blood. Her own responsiveness and their shared cravings for each other ...

His heart hurt and his chest felt caved in. He gasped for breath he couldn't find.

Willow.

No, please, no.

Surely the pain in his stomach would return any minute now and set him free from an entanglement he couldn't afford.

Surely.

He waited a minute ... five ... then ten. But for the first time in two-hundred years, since he'd risen to mastyr status, he had no pain. And from the events of the past two years and from the first time he chased Willow through the woods, it all made sense now, especially his complete and utter obsession with her.

There could be no doubt; Willow was his Goddess-be-damned blood rose.

He roared the depth of his frustration, letting his loneliness, his anger at the evil forces in his realm, and his blood-needs rage into the air. He was only surprised that the entire forest didn't catch fire with the depth of his distress.

When the last roar echoed down the hollows, he began coming back to himself.

Willow was a blood rose.

And nothing could change that.

The problem was that she could never be *his* blood rose.

He'd been in his recently built communication center and he'd read the exchanges of the bonded mastyrs, those who'd gone through exactly what he was experiencing, but who had also embraced their women. He knew the signs, especially the sudden release of centuries of terrible cramping in his stomach because only a blood rose could take that kind of pain away.

In his case, however, there were tough obstacles preventing him from ever bringing Willow fully into his life and he honestly didn't see how they could be overcome. His own duties demanded all of his time, and he couldn't be distracted by a woman. There was that. But worse, he'd played a terrible role in her father's death, so how would Willow ever be able to forgive him for what he'd done?

He cringed inwardly. The memories flooded back of when her father held a sharp blade to the troll's throat, threatening to kill him. Malik had tried to calm the grief-stricken husband down, but nothing could reach him. When the tall, fae professor sank the blade, cutting deep, he'd given Malik no choice; Malik had fired a single, powerful hand-blast straight into his head, killing him instantly.

The troll had almost died as a result of that cut.

Willow's fae father had essentially chosen death-by-Guardsman rather than live without his half-wraith, half-fae wife, leaving Willow orphaned.

And now the woman whose father he'd killed was his blood rose.

What a fucking nightmare.

Just when he was ready to release another set of roars, his phone rang. Pulling his cell from the pocket of his leathers, he was surprised to see that his housekeeper, Francesca, was calling him.

And she never called.

Sweet Goddess, what now?

"Francesca? What gives?"

"I am so sorry to bother you, Mastyr, but Davido is in your living room asking for you."

"Davido? The ancient troll who lives in Merhaine Realm?"

"Yes, that would be him. Davido the Wise. And he's pacing."

"He's pacing?" Malik tried to recall if he'd ever seen Davido *pace.*

"He seems sorely distressed, Mastyr, and can't raise you telepathically. He says he needs to speak to you at once."

At once. Holy shit. He glanced around. He'd flown two-hundred miles and was a helluva long way from his southern home. "I'll be there in twenty minutes."

"Can't you get here sooner? He has smoke rising from his elbows."

"I'll put on some speed."

~ ~ ~

Willow sat on the porch of her smaller meditation treehouse, a cup of cinnamon tea in hand. She wore a pair of jeans and a t-shirt, sitting with her knees up and her bare feet balanced on a footstool. She was listening to the night-birds chatter happily. An occasional bat flew by, something that always made her smile.

Bats were her particular friends, inclined as they were to swallow up insects by the ton-full each night. They kept her garden free of the small winged predators that could gobble up her fresh produce in a heartbeat.

She still had so much feel-good flowing through her veins that all she could do right now was smile. Of course, Malik had seemed distressed, but she knew that he'd deal with whatever was bothering him in his own time and way.

She sipped her tea and smiled a little more. She was in trouble. No question about that. But her veins had all these little joyful bursts of sensation exploding now and then to give her another dose of post-coital bliss.

She'd forgotten what it could be like or maybe she'd never really had this experience before, the savoring of sex with a man as powerful as Malik.

His shoulders. They were so well-muscled and yes, massive, even. She loved how he looked and felt physically, but then again what was not to love? He was a Vampire Guardsman, tall and built. His pecs were so beautiful that she wished she could call him back and spend some time feeling him up and maybe even sinking her wraith-fangs …

She caught her breath, closed her eyes, and forced the thoughts away or she'd be fully aroused all over again.

She'd meant for this to be nothing more than a first-and-a-last time with him, something to cleanse the palette so she could move on and return to her duties as the Protector of the wraith colony. Malik needed to become a distant memory.

She made herself relax and to release the images of him naked in her bed and on top of her, still joined. She wanted more, but she had to let him go.

What surprised her, as another sip of her tea brought the cinnamon sweetly into her mouth, was that she felt better, even stronger after having been with Malik. Maybe it was because she'd taken some of his blood, but she sensed that her ability to support the shield had improved.

Oh, but his blood. Dear sweet Goddess, the memory of not just his exquisite forest flavor, but of how she'd felt and how his blood had been like the most erotic fire down her throat, made her crave him all over again. And the more she'd suckled at his wrist, the more pleasure she'd felt deep inside her well.

If only she could be with him again.

But there was another obstacle besides her role as a Protector, which was something she needed to keep in the forefront of her mind. Malik was a Guardsman, and in many ways his lifestyle was opposed to her deeply committed fae life that always sought peace and a non-violent resolution to all problems.

Malik made war. He killed when necessary.

So, how could she ever be truly connected to all of that?

As the blissful sensations finally began to dim, and her responsibility as the Protector rose once more, she renewed her commitment. She knew her duty and she would fulfill the job given to her above all else.

And though she would always hold this night as one of the finest of her life, she had to let Malik go.

Taking a deep breath, she did just that.

As she stared out into the forest, however, she saw a faint light through all the branches and the leaves of the oak wood. Her heart set up a quick racket. No one should be able to find her here.

She tested the powerful spell that kept her home hidden in complete secrecy, and the charm held.

Malik had been able to see through the spell, but he was one of the most powerful vampires in the realm. Yet, as the light grew ever closer, she knew someone else had found her.

But who?

~ ~ ~

When Malik arrived back at his home in the south, his thoughts were divided between the reality about who Willow was in his life and the very bizarre fact that Davido was now in his home and very upset, at least according to his housekeeper.

Both circumstances had him tense as he entered the heavy, front door of his villa. He lived in a two-story house with an adjacent treehouse rec room that his Guardsmen could use whenever they wanted. The treehouse overlooked a fairly wide ravine, with a generous stream and a bathing pond.

When he didn't find Davido in his living room, he grew very still, extended his vampire hearing and listened for the old troll. The soft cursing that returned to him also surprised him as well as the location.

Davido was in his aviary of all places.

He crossed the living room and made his way through several smaller rooms to the path that led to the outdoor bird sanctuary. He'd never quite heard his birds squawking as much as they were right now.

Much of the hedge surrounding the aviary needed trimming back, so he couldn't see inside what was a large forested area covering a quarter acre. When he reached the entrance, and the cursing started again, he finally caught sight of Davido and laughed outright.

"What are you doing, my friend?"

Davido the Wise scowled at Malik since he had birds covering him from head-to-foot. It would appear that every bird in the aviary had taken a fancy to him. "This is my wife's doing. She took a pelter for reasons of which I am still ignorant. She gave me this spell insisting it would keep the birds away, but you see the true result for yourself." He made an odd, disparaging noise with his lips, worse than a simple raspberry.

Malik entered the screened gate and quickly shut it behind him. He watched the path carefully since many of the birds were injured and could only hop.

Tonight, apparently, he didn't need to worry; even the hopping birds climbed aboard the troll's feet.

Malik couldn't help but smile. "I didn't think it was possible for you to ever offend Vojalie, which means you must have really crossed the line with her. So what did you do?"

Davido shook his head, clearly bemused. "I only wish I knew. I'd apologize to her, a thousand fold, if I could figure out how I'd given offence."

Malik glanced around. Screen mesh covered the entire enclosure, preventing any of the birds from leaving and predators from getting inside. "So, why did you come to the aviary at all?"

He rolled his eyes. "Because of that damned spell. I was drawn here like a fly to gremlin shit."

The three rolls of his troll forehead were in such tight lines that Malik had the impression if Davido didn't get help soon, he'd burst into flames. And Francesca was right; he did have smoke coming out his elbows, a real sign he was quickly reaching his limit.

Malik sensed what needed to be done, having been the brunt of more than one of Alexandra the Bad's spells at one time or another. He drew close and, after gently nudging a chickadee out of the way first, he settled his hand on the troll's arm.

Just as Malik thought it would, the spell broke and the birds, one by one, fluttered away.

Davido's nostrils flared. "I need a fucking drink."

"Well, you've come to the right place, and I think I might just join you."

Once outside the aviary, Davido added, "Just to be clear, I want some of that fine Scottish single malt of yours."

"Absolutely. But we'll need to head to the treehouse."

Davido turned, glancing up into the canopy and glowering. "You mean the one up there?"

Malik glanced up at the large treehouse about fifty feet distant and nodded.

This time, Davido took hold of Malik's arm and said, "Hold on."

The next moment, Malik flew through some kind of space-time event. Only Davido and his wife Vojalie had the power to vanish and reappear in this way and this was the first time Malik had ever taken the trip himself.

He felt slightly disoriented as he arrived with Davido in the treehouse, a rec room he'd built just for his Guardsmen.

Davido looked around, still scowling. "A party pad for your Vampire Guard I see."

"Yep." Malik moved behind the bar and set out two glasses.

All the chairs were designed for big men and there was a pool table off to the side. A dozen stools lined the large bar.

He could hear splashing in the expansive pool below and the laughing of realm-women as they took advantage of the protected watering hole. The tree that housed the rec room had grown at the upper lip of the ravine through which a good sized stream flowed.

He'd had part of the stream dug out near the base of a twenty foot waterfall so that any females who wanted to partake could bathe freely without hindrance of clothes. Males of any species were forbidden to swim in the pool, but his Guardsmen had a view from above and could extend invitations to the women at will.

Malik turned and spun the combination to the safe that housed his liquor. Too many teenagers had taken advantage of the open nature of his treehouse and had pillaged his stock repeatedly.

Pouring out two glasses of Macallan and sliding one in Davido's direction, he said, "The truth is, I can't remember you ever having had a fight with your wife."

Davido and Vojalie were the model of domestic bliss.

"It's been a very long time since I felt her displeasure." He downed the first glass and pushed it forward, demanding a refill.

Davido rarely drank like this.

Malik was so shocked that for a long moment the glass he'd brought to his lips just rested there. Finally, he took a sip, then frowned at the ancient troll. "Well, you must have done something?" He poured out another two fingers for Davido.

"I can't think of a damn thing. All I know is that my wife had some sort of vision in which I did something she didn't like, something she said was very crude, and she was all over my troll ass for it. I think it highly unfair that any man be held accountable for something in a vision until that 'something' happens. But she was breathing fire when I left to come here."

Malik shook his head. "And is that why you've come?"

"Oh, for fuck's sake no. That's not the reason. What do you take me for, a gremlin's hind end?"

Malik threw back the rest of his drink and decided that given all that had happened, he needed another one. Pouring out his second, he then waggled the bottle at Davido. "Want another one, my friend?"

"Hell, yes. Three fingers, this time. I'm not going home until I'm blasted out of my head."

Given that Malik had just learned that he now had a blood rose who he didn't want, he joined Davido until the pair of them were seated in adjacent chairs with the bottle on the low table in front of them, and a whole lot of slurring going on.

Malik had his fifth drink in hand as he said, "Found two dead children earlier this evening. Just about lost my shit. And this lovely troll cleaned all the blood from my uniform while I stood there in shock."

"Sweet Goddess," Davido murmured. "I'm reminded of that human earth-saying that sometimes life just sucks."

Davido continued to drink.

Malik kept the scotch flowing.

Finally, Davido said, "But I can't forget why I came here …. which is … oh, shit. Now I'm remembering, and it's bad, my friend. Bad." He reached over and grabbed Malik's arm. "I'm sorry to tell you this, but you have to bond with Willow. She's your blood rose, which I sense you already know. But she's more than that. She has a connection to the absolute heart of our world, and though I'm not given much to prophesying...." He hiccupped and worked a little harder at getting out what he wanted to say. "Right now the entire future of the Nine Realms depends on you getting into that woman's sweet spot and staying there."

Had Davido just said 'sweet spot'?

Malik didn't know how to respond, because he was completely torn between two powerful reactions. The first caused all his muscles to tense up since he was ready to beat the troll to a pulp for even mentioning Willow's 'sweet spot'. The other filled Malik with an absolute horror that the fate of the entire Nine Realms – not just Ashleaf, but all Nine – now sat on his already overburdened shoulders.

He decided that since Davido was fairly trashed, he'd let the comment slide about Willow's female parts. "You have no idea what I'm dealing with here. The Society just killed another family, and I intend to start relocating every half-breed in my realm to Swanicott Island."

"Why?"

Okay, Davido was seriously drunk.

The troll turned toward the part of the treehouse that overlooked the stream. The entire rec room was open to the air, and each wall was built up only half way which offered a proper view of the surroundings. A few more stools lined the ravine side.

"And what is that delightful sound, like chimes tinkling? Am I hearing the laughter of women? I'm enraptured." He set his drink down and slid off the chair. He took three steps, almost toppled over, then weaved his way to the half-wall.

Leaning against the edge, he peered down into the pool below. He whistled, then called out over his shoulder. "Why haven't you invited me here … " he belched, "before. This is a visual feast. Sunny-side-up eggs all floating in the water. I'm enchanted."

Malik set his drink down. The image that now moved through his mind of women baring their breasts, plus the fact that he was half in the bag, prompted him to join Davido.

Taking up a stool next to the troll, Malik released a heavy sigh. The sight of so much skin, however, took him straight back to being with Willow. He even felt guilty as he stared down at the bathers.

Davido whistled again and whispered, "Look at the hooters on that one. She'd have to have her lady garments special made. Float for me, sweetheart. Yeah, that's it. On your back. Oh, yeah."

A feminine voice called up to him, "Davido the Wise, is that you? Why, you haven't been to my bar in a goat's age? How are you, my fine troll?"

Davido leaned over the railing now, his inhibitions completely wiped out by the Macallan. He opened his mouth to speak, but a woman's voice coming from behind him and strident in tone, disrupted the moment.

"Just as I thought! My visions never lie. And here you are, flirting with another woman."

Davido whirled around, then fell right on his ass next to Malik's stool. "My love," he slurred.

"You're drunk?"

Malik quickly left his stool and crossed to Vojalie, although he swayed a couple of times in making the effort. With long dark brown hair and large, expressive brown eyes, Vojalie was absolutely one of the most beautiful fae women in the Nine Realms. She carried her toddler, an adorable troll child, Bernice, on her hip.

"Hello, Vojalie." Malik struggled to put his words in order. "It's so nice to see you. Sorry, the inebriation is my fault. He was pretty upset when he arrived."

Vojalie huffed a sigh. "He should have been, because I told him this would happen."

Malik stared at Davido now struggling to his feet. "That he'd get drunk in my rec room and flirt with naked women?" Somewhere in the back of his mind, he knew he wasn't helping Davido's cause.

"They're naked?"

Malik felt a warmth climb his cheeks. "Uh, it's something I sanctioned. Uh … " No possible justification came into his head, so he shut the hell up.

"Hi," Bernice said, her head burrowed against her mother's neck. Her hair was a beautiful pile of soft, black curls.

Malik smiled and held out his arms to the child. The troll toddler smiled back then went to him. For reasons Malik had never understood, children tended to like and trust him and right now, he went with it. "I'll take her flying, if that's okay." Kids loved to fly.

"One moment." Vojalie planted a hand firmly on top of his head. Sudden healing waves flowed through his brain, completely reversing the effects of the alcohol. "I have a great deal of respect for you, Malik, but you're not flying my child anywhere when you can't even walk a straight line."

"You did the right thing." Glancing at Davido, he added, "I'll take her to the aviary to see the birds."

"That might be best."

He switched to levitation, moved over to the right side of the platform, then launched to fly along the path that led to the bird sanctuary.

Bernice giggled her approval, clearly enjoying levitated flight. Once inside the aviary, the birds fluttered and hopped nearby, hoping for some extra seed. Dozens of Ashleaf night-birds lived within the sanctuary, each a different species and in every color of the rainbow, some with pronounced plumage, others with short bright crowns.

He'd made one complete circuit when Vojalie and Davido joined him. Davido had sobered up as well.

Vojalie explained, "All is settled between us, Malik, and I do apologize since I believe the fault may have been mine. Davido wouldn't have gotten drunk if I hadn't gotten angry and put that bird-spell on him. I was part of the problem and I admit it."

Davido, holding his wife's hand, looked up at her, "And I apologize again for leering at that troll, my love. Unconscionable."

"You are very forgiven, my sweet, and you were quite right; those were a massive pair of knockers." She leaned down and kissed Davido, an expression of affection that went on and on.

Malik took Bernice on a second tour of the aviary.

After a good ten minutes of the sound of distant cooing between husband and wife, Malik heard Vojalie call to him. "Malik, you must come here. I have something to tell you."

He returned quickly, by which time Bernice had seen enough of the aviary and wanted her mother's arms.

Gathering the toddler back to her hip, Vojalie said, "I hadn't planned on joining Davido on this trip, but as soon as he left I had another vision, which was almost violent in nature in terms of sensation."

Malik wasn't sure just how much more he could take. His night had begun with a terrible murder, followed by an overwhelming experience in Willow's bed. And after realizing she was his blood rose, he'd had to contend with Davido's insistence that the destiny of the Nine Realms would depend on his bonding with Willow.

He drew a deep breath. "What did you see?"

"I know there must be some sort of interpretation but not a single one of my usually competent fae intuitions could explain why the very center of your realm explodes in a burst of white light."

"What?" His voice sounded dull to his own ears. "What on earth do you mean?" He shook his head several times. "Are you speaking about the end of the Nine Realms? Or just Ashleaf?"

Davido had drawn close to Vojalie and now had his arm around her waist. He had never appeared more serious as he once more looked up at her. "Yes, my love, I beg you will be more forthcoming. You have left even your husband shaking on his powerful troll legs."

Vojalie frowned and shook her head. "I only wish I knew what to tell you because I have no real sense of the meaning. I can only report what I saw?"

Malik asked, "Can you at least tell me if the vision suggested something evil in this explosion? Will this be the work of one of my enemies? Or even Margetta?"

Vojalie sighed, settling into her shoulders. "I just don't know, but I promise you that if I should learn something more I will contact Alexandra the Bad and have her relay the information. Or I'll come myself, or Davido will."

"And when does this event take place?"

Vojalie merely shrugged. "I'm sorry. I have no idea."

When Bernice put her hand on Vojalie's face and made a whimpering sound, even Malik understood that the youngster had had her fill of the visit.

Vojalie kissed Bernice on the forehead. "I need to get her home."

Malik nodded. He promised that he would think carefully about what each had told him. After an exchange of farewells, the couple vanished. He stared at the empty space, wondering what the hell it meant that part of his realm would explode into a ball of white light.

~ ~ ~

Willow had exhausted herself raising shields against the small roving light that had drawn so close to her treehouse complex. She had no idea who the entity could be but feared that it was Margetta, also known as the Ancient Fae, the woman who had created the Invictus centuries ago.

Though the entity kept tapping on her mind, trying to gain entrance, she blocked her telepathy. She had no idea who had come to her home.

Finally, when a severe headache threatened, she allowed the telepathic communication.

Willow, I do beg your pardon for coming unannounced, but I had to speak with you.

Willow sank back into her wooden porch chair. *Illiandra, thank the Goddess, it's you. But please tell me that you are nearby because all I can see is a small white light in the distance?*

Yes, I'm about thirty feet away, and I have a flashlight because I've had the worst time finding your home.

Willow explained. *It's under a protective spell, but why didn't you tell me you were coming?* Willow had an understanding with Illiandra that her visits would always be prearranged.

There wasn't time to take the usual careful measures. I've had a vision.

Willow groaned inwardly. Now, what?

She removed the charm and a few seconds later, Illiandra floated through the woods straight for the meditation porch.

Illiandra had assumed a fae form, something most pure-blood wraiths could do, even when they didn't bear fae blood. She landed lightly on the wood porch.

Willow's gaze went immediately to the woman's throat and upper chest since she bore a natural ring of feathers that had sprouted like a necklace, the coloration varying from magenta, to green, to a deep navy blue. It was one of the most beautiful realm-attributes that existed.

Not all wraiths produced a ring of feathers, only the most powerful, like Illiandra.

Willow moved toward her. "I'm so sorry for the confusion."

Illiandra held out both hands and Willow took them. She kissed Willow on each cheek, her scent delicate like a lightly fragranced powder. Her gown was made of silk in a soft ivory and cut low to showcase the feathers, and her blond hair was piled on top of her head in a series of intricate braids. Soft bands of eye-shadow complemented the feathers in matching colors. She was exquisite.

"So tell me about this vision that prompted you to leave the colony."

"In a moment, but first I must know a few things." Illiandra held her gaze firmly and Willow felt a dizziness roll through her mind.

The wraith had tremendous power, and using her enthrallment skills she searched through Willow's recent memories.

When she released Willow's hands, she blinked. "You've made love with Mastyr Malik."

What else could Willow say? "Yes, recently."

"This is most fortuitous, but might we talk for a few minutes?"

Willow didn't spend a lot of time in the wraith-colony for the same reason she didn't often go out and about in Ashleaf; she had to retain her focus at all costs.

But she'd forgotten how polite the wraiths were in general, never wanting to intrude, which was one more reason that Mastyr Axton's campaign to rid Ashleaf of all wraiths was so absurd. Most wraiths, so long as they were unaffected by Margetta's horrible taint, were kind and gentle.

"Of course, but why don't we retire to my study and I'll prepare us some tea."

"That would be delightful."

"Do you still prefer chamomile?"

"I do."

Later, settled with a stoneware teacup in hand, Illiandra glanced around the study. "I do love this room. You have so many books. Have you read them all?"

"Yes. It is my favorite thing."

Illiandra nodded and sipped her tea. She released a sigh. "I suppose you must be wondering what prompted me to come here, but I had to speak with you, and I couldn't raise you telepathically. Of course, with all these spells in place, I now understand why."

A jolt of anxiety hit Willow. "Tell me what's happened?"

"There is no easy way to say this, but the breach that the colony suffered recently has had an effect, which is something our seers have witnessed in a shared vision. They've seen a dark cloud that now overshadows the entrance to the colony where Mastyr Axton attempted to break through with his illegal charm."

Willow leaned forward. "I want to assure you that the entrance shield holds. I restored it completely."

"I know you did."

"But now you believe Axton will attack again?"

"I'm convinced he will."

Willow's heart sank further. "Do you think he's in league with someone?"

Holding her cup in the palm of her hand, Illiandra gently swirled her tea then drank. "I have no idea but there are a number of powerful fae who specialize in illegal charms, selling them on the black market all through the Nine Realms. Any of these could have sold the charm to Axton."

Willow had repulsed him once, having been equal to the task, but what if he purchased a more powerful charm? She truly didn't think she could counteract anything stronger.

Setting her teacup aside, she rubbed her forehead. "There's something you need to know, Mistress. I feel as though I've reached a limit in what I can perform in terms of my Protector service. I've found it increasingly difficult in recent years to sustain what I do for the colony.

"In the beginning, I was able to enjoy a great number of activities while holding the shield intact. But that's not so anymore. I feel as though I'm in constant danger of losing my grip on the power I stream."

Illiandra settled her hand on Willow's arm. "Why, with all that's holy in our realm, did you not tell me sooner?"

"I don't know. It happened so gradually that I just accepted it as my job. But when Axton attacked the vines, I could feel that I'd reach a critical limit."

Illiandra leaned back in her chair and set the teacup and saucer aside. She fell into a contemplative state and Willow had enough sense to let her be.

The woman and her husband, Gervassay, had led the wraith colony for at least two millennia, which was long before Willow was born. She had met them on the first day of her service and considered them to be two of the wisest realm-folk she'd ever known. Nothing but kindness ever flowed from their tongues.

Finally, Illiandra shifted slightly toward Willow. "I greatly fear that events have coalesced that will change Ashleaf forever. Our future rests on the head of a pin and can fall through the winds of fate either for good or for evil.

"I also fear that much rests on your shoulders, Willow, and I'm sorry for that because you have lain down your life for the colony, sacrificing year after year with no thought for your personal needs or desires.

"Though I am reluctant to say as much, I believe that our only hope is for you to bond with Mastyr Malik. In that bond, you may find the power you need."

Willow didn't understand. "I'm confused. What do you mean that I should bond with Malik? We shared a lovely moment together, but it was for the purpose of ending things, not beginning anything."

"Oh, dear. You don't know, do you? You don't realize what you are?"

Willow shook her head. "I know exactly what I am. I am the Protector."

But Illiandra just looked at Willow, forcing her to think, but to ponder what? That it had something to do with Malik was clear, yet she had no clue as to which direction her thoughts should take.

Then she recalled the very moment when Malik had grown distressed a few minutes after their lovemaking. In fact, he'd appeared as though he'd been struck hard in the chest.

Realm-folk often engaged in bonding through their mating vibrations, especially in marriage. And even several of the Realm rulers had bonded, but their mates were blood roses, which was a recent and very bizarre phenomenon of the Nine Realms.

She shook her head briskly back and forth several times, then murmured out loud, "No."

"Yes," Illiandra countered.

Willow once again recalled the look on Malik's face. Had he touched his stomach? Had he realized he had no pain? Had her blood resolved two centuries of the horrible cramping that accompanied chronic blood-starvation in mastyr vampires? Was that what had upset him? That he'd realized she was a blood rose?

Once more, she shook her head. "You think I have this new gift — the one that's meant to relieve mastyr vampires of their suffering?"

Illiandra nodded slowly. "I do. Have you not *craved* Mastyr Malik?"

Willow felt ill. She didn't want yet another powerful and difficult gift that would bind her in service to Ashleaf Realm. Protecting the wraith colony was enough.

She rose to her feet and for a moment couldn't catch her breath. "I can't do this. I can't. You have no idea how hard just tending the colony is. I don't have time, or energy, or power or anything."

"Was making love with Malik so draining then?"

Willow could hardly put two thoughts together. "No, quite the opposite. I … I felt powerful afterwards."

Illiandra rose to her feet as well. "You have a lot to think about. Unfortunately, my intuition tells me you will not have a lot of time to process what has happened. I am sorry, Willow, and I hope that as the next few hours unfold, you'll find your way to making peace with the mastyr. But now, I must return. I have a meeting with the Elders in a few minutes. Just think about these things and if you can, prepare yourself."

Illiandra then transformed to her wraith form and floated through the open window of the study, afterward disappearing from sight.

Willow wasn't certain whether she was distressed that Illiandra had left her so abruptly, or grateful she was gone. At least now she could perhaps pretend that her world hadn't just crashed all around her.

Carrying both sets of empty teacups and saucers back to the kitchen, Willow busied herself with cleaning up. Maybe if she soaped up the cups, rinsed them and dried them, she'd realize that the last couple of hours had been a dream. She'd wake up and maybe spend some time working in her garden.

But by the time she'd put the tea things away, her heart had grown heavy with the recent revelations. And as she pondered her entire relationship with Malik, as well as his sudden reactions after their lovemaking, she knew she was exactly what Illiandra said she was: *a blood rose.*

Tears bit her eyes. But what about her own desires of what she wanted for her life? Then it occurred to her that she had no life. She hadn't truly enjoyed her existence from the time that she'd maxed out her power safeguarding the colony. And if she couldn't even support the colony shield, how was she supposed to add to her duties if she became bonded to the mastyr?

As she moved into the living room, however, a wave a dizziness assaulted her, forcing her to her knees. A moment later, she rolled onto her back to lie prone on the floor.

A vision was on her, profound and vital.

She'd half expected to see Malik and to witness their bonding or something similar.

Instead, Axton came into view, and this time, he carried with him a much larger charm made up of glowing emeralds.

In the Nine Realms, emeralds had the ability to carry great power, which was why she knew this charm was special and much stronger than the last one.

He approached the entrance to the colony and closed his eyes, connecting with the charm. And just like that, the vines began to melt away, while smoke rose high into the air as the charm did its work.

The vision ended as abruptly as it arrived. She sat up, feeling sick at heart all over again.

Struggling to her feet, she realized there was only one person she could call, and he was the last person right now she wanted to see. But it couldn't be helped. If Axton was coming after the wraith colony, she would need help stopping him.

She crossed to the coffee table and picked up her cellphone. When Malik answered, she bit back her tears. "I've had a vision and, Malik, my wraiths are in terrible trouble. I need your help."

Malik's quick response squeezed her heart hard. "Of course, Willow. Anything."

Chapter Four

Malik would swear Willow was in tears, but why? And what was happening to her wraiths? "You sound really upset."

"I'm overwhelmed, but I'll come around."

"Tell me what's happened."

She spoke quickly about a vision that involved Axton using a charm to burn through the vines that guarded the wraith families. "I believe he's intent on murdering the wraiths."

"And the vision was just about Axton?"

"Yes, but he had an extremely powerful, and very illegal, charm made up of emeralds. Malik, I need your help. If he breaks through the entrance, he'll attack the wraiths, the families."

Malik had no doubt that Willow had seen a vision that would be coming true anytime now. And even though both Vojalie and Davido had given him enough information to send him in Willow's direction, he wasn't ready. He wanted time to figure things out, to perhaps talk to Alexandra the Bad and see if he had another recourse with Willow.

At this point, he wasn't even sure Willow knew what she was, and given the stress in her voice, he didn't exactly want to bring the subject up. "Give me a minute."

"Of course."

He held the phone away, pressing it against his thigh. He recalled that Davido had said the future of the Nine Realms hung in the balance and that in Davido's opinion, Malik needed to bond with Willow if his world had any chance of survival. And what the hell had Vojalie's vision been about, the one involving an explosion of white light?

Overwhelmed was right.

He drew the phone back up to his ear. "Willow, are you acting on just the information from the vision?"

"No. A powerful, um, realm person came to visit me as well, one from … the north."

"Which realm person?"

"I can't say. It's part of the deal I made when I agreed to protect these families."

"The deal? I don't understand."

"I … I can't explain it right now. I'm just asking you to come to me, to help me deal with Axton when he shows up." She paused for a moment, then, "Please, Malik. I need you to do this for me. So many lives depend on keeping Axton from breaching the entrance. I was able to stop him before, but I don't think I can do it again, not after what I saw in the vision."

"What do you mean, 'before'?"

"It was last night and he had a charm then, but I didn't know what to make of it. At the time, I had sufficient power to stop him, but not for the one in the vision, at least not by myself. I'll need him physically stopped, then I can heal the vines because that's what the charm does, it destroys the vines."

"Willow, why didn't you tell me this earlier?"

"Because I was trying to keep everything secret, which is what the wraith families want."

Knowing that the vision constituted a second event, Malik had no problem believing his assistance was critical, so he made his decision quickly. "I'll be right there, but where do you want me? At the vines?"

"Can you come back to my house?"

His heart kicked into high gear.

Back to her house, to the place he'd made love to her.

In a sudden swell of unexpected sensation, he forgot all about how much he resented the sudden appearance of a blood rose in his life. Instead, he focused on the other side of the coin, that he really liked this woman. Making love with her had been one of the best experiences of his entire life and not just because of the insane attraction, but because she'd taken the time to bathe him.

He didn't think he would ever forget what he felt like in that moment, as though treated with great value. She'd honored him more than just a man who could give her pleasure, but someone she trusted and respected.

"I'll be there as quickly as I can."

Before he left, he filled Evan in on most of what he'd just gone through, choosing to reveal the existence of several wraith families hidden on Willow's land. He needed at least one member of his Vampire Guard to be aware of the recent fast-moving events. "I think you'd better put the Guard on alert. Let them know that our pal Axton has been purchasing illegal charms in order to find wraiths he intends to murder."

"Sweet Goddess, how long has Willow been hiding wraiths?"

"I think this has been going on for decades."

"But this makes no sense. I mean, how could *you* not have known?"

And here was a big truth. "Because Willow has tremendous power, more than I've seen in even Alexandra the Bad. I believe she might have as much ability as Vojalie, or damn close."

Evan whistled. "And where do you want me?"

"Just stick close to your phone or if you feel me battering your telepathic frequency, let me in."

"You got it, boss."

When Malik hung up, he slid his phone deep into the pocket of his leathers, then let his housekeeper know he was headed north again. He swept into the cool night air, flying high above the forest canopy.

When he arrived at Willow's main treehouse, he saw her first before she saw him. She was sitting on her front porch, elbows on knees, head in hands. Boy, could he relate.

"Willow," he called softly as he landed on the wood deck.

She sat up, pushing her long, red hair away from her face. She wore a tank-top and jeans again and looked amazing. Yeah, he had it bad.

"You look … so beautiful." He hadn't meant to speak the words out loud, but that's exactly what had flipped through his mind.

She stood up. "Thank you." But her brow was furrowed and her eyes looked a little red-rimmed.

A strange sensation moved through him, and he acted on it. Stepping close, he took her in his arms and just like that she came to him and sank against his chest. "This has been too much."

His heart squeezed up tight as he held her. "I couldn't agree more." It occurred to him that Willow might have learned the truth about herself as well. "When this realm-person came to see you, did she have other things to tell you as well?"

He felt Willow sigh heavily. "You mean, that I'm a blood rose?"

Somehow, it made it much easier to have their shared reality hit the air. "Yes, that bizarre thing that is affecting both of us."

She drew back to look at him, but didn't pull out of his arms. "You knew, didn't you, after we'd made love?"

He nodded. "I suspected, because I had no more pain. It's unbelievable."

"I'm sorry, Malik. I had no idea. I would never have asked you over earlier if I'd understood what I was. This must feel like some kind of trap to you."

"I suspect we're both feeling trapped, but I certainly don't blame you. Willow, please know that. If anything, it explains my drive toward you, why I couldn't keep away, and why I would chase you to the entrance to your land every time. I was obsessed, but now it makes sense."

She eased away from him and folded her arms over her stomach. "I don't want to be this thing."

"You don't?"

She stared at him. "No, of course not. I have enough to do with protecting these … families."

All this time, since he'd left her, his thoughts had been focused solely on himself and not on how the nature of her current gift would affect her. "Shit."

"What? Why did you say that?" Her auburn brows rose.

"I just realized that you'll be sought after by other mastyr vampires."

"What do you mean?"

"Your blood rose gift isn't specific to me."

"You mean I'll be pursued by all mastyrs?" She shuddered visibly. "I don't think I get this. I've seen several mastyrs in the various villages around Ashleaf, but no one has come after me. Only you."

At that, he smiled. "Well, maybe because I was the only one powerful enough to see through your charms."

She offered a half-smile in return. "That would explain it, I guess. But why now? I mean, was I always a blood rose? I'm not sure how this works."

Malik shrugged. "From the conversations I've had with several of the bonded mastyrs, the woman's gift just sort of comes online, but at what point is unclear."

She frowned as though working hard to understand. "Well, maybe that point for me was seeing you on market day at Cherry Hollow."

"I know that's when it all started for me. But you'll need to be careful, Willow, because you'll want to feed other mastyr vampires until you've completed the bond."

Her eyes went wide. "You mean until I'm bonded to you or some other mastyr these powerful cravings will just go on and on?"

He nodded. "I think that's the way it works."

She covered her mouth with both hands. "No, sweet Goddess, no." She then tossed her hands wide. "Dammit, this just keeps getting worse."

Malik was so surprised by her uncharacteristic outburst that he chuckled. "I think that's better."

"What? That I said 'dammit'?"

"Maybe, because this situation is really twisted."

"Yes, it is. I was barely holding on and now I'm supposed to do what?" She tossed her hand in his direction, almost slapping his chest. "Serve your every need, every desire? I mean, come on."

At that, he laughed. "I don't think being a blood rose means that you serve a mastyr in that way. I don't think that's the point."

"Well, what is the point? I'd be servicing your blood-needs on demand."

At that, other powerful images shot through his mind and being the male that he was, he drew close and caught the back of her arm. "And I could service yours as well, remember that. I loved it when you took from my wrist. I'd love to have you taking more of my life-force and from other places as well."

Willow blinked several times slowly. If he'd been afraid that he'd overstepped the line, the sudden rise of her fresh forest-rain scent allayed his fears. The sexual component to the blood rose phenomenon was very mutual, something he'd experienced with her starting about two years ago when he'd seen her, just as she'd said, in Cherry Hollow.

For a long moment, she remained staring into his eyes, her breathing shallow. Finally, she said, "It was wonderful to take from your wrist and afterward I did feel a measure of power. Your blood did something to me."

"Really?"

"Yes. And the sex. Malik, it was the most amazing experience."

"I felt so caught up I forgot where I was. And the vines! Sweet Goddess, don't get me started on your vine ability. The vines tightened and held us together, but they moved with us as well." He lowered his voice, "It was hot as hell."

At that, she smiled, her eyes glittering, and his chest started to hurt all over again.

Willow did something to him, something more significant than just her blood rose gift that had ended his chronic starvation. He liked her and respected her. He enjoyed being with her now that they were talking, interacting.

And for just a second, he allowed himself to wonder what it would be like to have her in his life from this point forward, to have a woman share his bed, his worries, his table. He'd been so long without a companion in his life that he found the idea far more seductive than anything else in this situation.

So how long had he been feeling that kind of emptiness in his night-to-night routine? Of course, he never allowed himself to think in those terms. The mastyrs who ruled each of the Nine Realms rarely had long-term anything, since Margetta had unleashed her Invictus wraith-pairs onto their world.

But the blood rose phenomenon had changed all that. And now he was here, staring at his own blood rose and wondering if he could make a life with Willow.

He let go of her arm, knowing that they had tough issues to face, including what to do about Axton.

That bastard. And now he was infringing on the property rights of one of his fellow citizens by purchasing illegal charms. Apparently, the murderer in him couldn't rest so long as a single wraith existed in Ashleaf.

"Where did you go just now?" Willow asked.

He turned back to her. "Just thinking about Axton and our current dilemma. But how did Axton learn that you had wraiths on your land?"

"I honestly don't know, although my best guess is that the same fae who has prepared illegal and highly potent charms for him may have also had a vision of the wraith families."

"You're probably right."

"Malik, just how dangerous is Axton? I don't really know him at all. Battling his spell was the closest contact I've ever had with him."

Malik thought for a moment, searching for the exact right words to describe him. "It's true that Axton was enraged when the Sidhe Council approved me as Mastyr of Ashleaf once I came into my mastyr power. And you could also say that his motivation to somehow find a way to take Ashleaf back rules his life.

"But I've known him a long time, and I've come to believe there's something more here than meets the eye. He's ambitious, yes, but the truth is that he could have assassinated me anytime he wanted over the past two centuries, yet he didn't. Instead, he created The Society not just to kill the innocent, but to create terror and chaos as well."

"Do you think he's a psychopath?"

"I believe that would be accurate. But I'd like you to consider looking at this problem in a different way because there's a simple solution. Let's relocate the families on your land to Swanicott Island, in Mastyr Zane's realm. There is a large pure-blood wraith population living there and your families would be welcome and more importantly, they'd be safe."

Once more, she tightened her arms around her stomach. "I honestly don't think they'd ever want to leave Ashleaf Realm."

"But it would be for the best since it's clear that Axton is after them."

"I know, but these families have a profound connection to their land."

Malik narrowed his eyes. He sensed she was holding something back, but he was reluctant to press her. She'd already been through so much and there would be plenty of time to discuss the relocation process.

"Why don't I meet these families and see what they think? Willow, I promise you that I do know the difference between the Invictus wraith-pairs that Margetta has created and a solid wraith family working the land."

At that, she met his gaze and a soft smile curved her lips. "I know you do. I don't doubt that for a second."

"Then you'll let me talk to them?"

She looked away from him for a long moment as though weighing the issue. When she shifted her gaze back to his, she said, "I think it might be for the best. You rule this realm and you should know what's going on." Suddenly, she put a hand to her chest. "Malik, I can feel a new charm at work trying to break through the shield."

"You mean right now? Do you think Axton is back at the vines?"

He watched tears fill her eyes. "He is. And that charm … sweet Goddess, it's so powerful."

"Fuck." Malik nodded several times. "I'll want back up. Give me a sec."

He shifted his focus to Evan, and because he needed to supply coordinates mentally, Malik contacted him mind-to-mind.

Evan, I'm going to need your help, but first, is everything okay with the Vampire Guard? Malik's adrenaline pumped hard.

We're good here. No Invictus sign, but I can hear shit in your voice. What's going on?

Trouble on Willow's land. Axton procured another illegal charm and is trying to dislodge the wraith families I told you about.

That motherfucker. Where do you want us and how many?

Bring two squads with you.

You got it.

Eight vampire Guardsmen should be enough to take care of Axton. He mentally sent the location and disconnected.

To Willow, he said, "You'll need to release your protective charm over your gate, or my men won't be able to get in. Please tell me it's separate from the one that keeps the wraith families hidden."

"It is." She closed her eyes and he could feel a rolling sensation as the charm disappeared. Opening her eyes, she nodded. "Done."

"Let me fly you to Axton's position."

"I was hoping you'd say that, but skip the paths and head into the sky."

"You just read my mind."

He gestured to his right boot, and when she stepped up and slung an arm around his neck, he took to the air.

~ ~ ~

Willow leaned her head close to Malik, nestling against his shoulder. She wasn't used to flying with vampires and wanted to be sure she made it easy for him to maneuver.

But as Malik lifted above the forest canopy and moved swiftly to the west in the direction of the colony, she felt as though she'd dropped into a warm bath and wanted to stay there forever. With the need to make sure her wraiths were safe, she'd forgotten how much she desired him, a sensation reinforced by the fact that she was essentially held tightly in his arms.

Desire flowed as it always did, yet so inappropriately given the situation that her cheeks warmed yet again.

Forcing her attention to the matter at hand, she focused on her protective shield and the battering it was now taking. And the closer Malik flew to the colony, the stronger the charm's vibration beat against her mind.

She felt someone tapping against her telepathy as well and because she was away from the protective charms surrounding her treehouse residence, she tested the frequency and felt Illiandra trying to reach her.

Willow, we're under attack again.

I'm on it, she pathed.

Hurry. The charm is much more powerful than the last one and Axton is almost through.

We're just a few seconds out.

We?

Mastyr Malik and I.

Oh, thank the Goddess. He'll be able to help you. I just know it.

Illiandra shut down the communication as Malik dropped ten feet behind Axton, releasing Willow at once.

Axton stood outside the entrance to the colony. Smoke streamed into the air as the vines burned. The rancid smell was almost more than Willow could bear.

Malik shouted, "What the fuck do you think you're doing, Axton?"

Startled, Axton turned to glare at Malik over his shoulder, his gaze skating over Willow, then returning to Malik. But he kept the charm on full bore. "There are wraiths behind this protective shield and I intend to expose them."

"Oh, you do, do you?"

Willow was about to mention to Malik that he needed to stop Axton from using the charm, when Malik suddenly closed the distance, drew back his arm and punched Axton in the jaw. When Axton flew backward, he lost control of the charm and the large, glowing emeralds fell to the ground. Malik didn't hesitate to grind each gemstone into the dirt with the heel of his boot.

The charm broke instantly.

Willow had never really seen any of the Guardsmen in action before, so watching Malik take charge as swiftly as he did stunned her. Witnessing this side of him caused her interest to rise yet another notch. Of course, he was a man of war, and he'd chosen the simplest route to disarming the situation. But it had worked.

The vines called to her suddenly, a soft frequency reminding her that she had a job to do.

She slipped past Malik and melted into the wounded vines. She ignored the smell and quickly began the healing process. Releasing her power in a steady wave, the stench dissipated swiftly as the vines regenerated at lightning speed.

At the same time, she could see and hear both men. Axton had gained his feet and stood with his fists at his side, his neck arched forward as he confronted Malik.

The leader of The Society had dark, almost black eyes and a feral look that had always given her the creeps. He was Guardsman height, though not as tall as Malik and had thick light red hair that he wore short and shaved close on one side. Though predominately vampire, his sharp chin spoke of a partial fae heritage. His unusually pale skin and bony look indicated a use of cocaine, one of the imports from the States that had afflicted at least one percent of the realm population.

"Where did that woman – that fae – go? Is she the one protecting these wraiths?"

"You're on a need-to-know basis, and right now you don't fucking need to know. You're trespassing."

At that moment, at least eight of the Vampire Guard floated in from the canopy above, descending to form a half circle around Axton. One of them she knew as Evan, Malik's right arm.

"Couldn't handle this alone?" Axton spat on the ground.

"Just wanted witnesses to your crime. You've broken two of our laws: the illegal use of fae charms and being on private property without permission. I can arrest you or you can keep the hell away from here from now on. Which will it be?"

Willow understood exactly why Malik wasn't in a hurry to arrest Axton. The vampire was a pro at using the media for his own purposes and wouldn't hesitate to exploit an arrest to his advantage. The Society would go to work as well, spreading its hate propaganda all around the realm until Willow would end up with a mob at her gates and more dead half-breeds.

But for a split-second, she had a terrible feeling that putting Axton in jail was exactly what Malik should do.

Axton sniffed long and loud, a by-product of using the white powder. "You're missing the point, Malik, as you always do. This woman is hiding wraiths on her land, wraiths that could easily become Invictus."

"And I think you're missing the point. You're trespassing."

Axton took a step toward Malik. "I've done more for Ashleaf than you ever will. I'm hunting wraiths, a service I performed long before you arrived and the reason our realm has the lowest percentage of Invictus attacks than any of the other realms. The people you serve know it and one day there will be hell to pay. You'll see."

Willow thought Axton was the consummate hypocrite and that Malik had called it right; Axton's mind was bent. He was a real sociopath, seeing life through the prism of his own perverted ambitions.

The vines were now fully healed and the entrance to the colony protected once more. Willow could have remained in the safety of her invisibility, but everything was changing and instinctively she felt she needed to be part of the stand against Axton. She also thought it would be wise for Malik's Guardsmen to see what she could do because every particle of her being told her that what had happened here tonight was just the beginning. Axton all but vibrated with his determination to get at the wraiths.

She emerged from the vines which brought a few 'holy shits' moving through the gathered Guardsmen.

"You're back," Axton said, but as he stared at her, a frown formed between his dark, angled brows. "And where exactly did you go?"

"I repaired the vines."

"How?" But even as the word left Axton's mouth, he got a funny look on his face as his gaze bored into hers. "By all the elf lords, I can smell what you are. Holy fuck. You're a goddess-be-damned blood rose."

Malik tensed beside her. "It's none of your business what Willow is. Now get the hell out of here." He even moved to position himself slightly in front of her.

Willow suddenly understood the mistake she'd made by emerging before Axton left, but it was too late.

Though she stood close to Malik, her blood rose drive to feed all mastyr vampires roared to life until she was completely focused on Axton. To her horror, she realized she was drawn to him for the sole reason that he was a mastyr vampire and she was a blood rose.

His eyes glinted and he angled his head in a way she could only describe as predatory. Yet, she liked it, liked him for looking at her. "So, what's your name, Mistress?"

"Willow." The part of her rational mind that still worked, despised that she could be drawn to him on any level, yet she was.

"I don't recall seeing you around Ashleaf. You must be new to these parts." Even his voice sounded seductive to her receptive ears.

Because Willow's mind had shifted its focus and she began picking up on Axton's mastyr frequency, she didn't quite get the affect this exchange was having on Malik. In fact, she'd all but forgotten he was there, until he caught her arm and turned her toward him, breaking her mounting drive toward Axton.

His fangs sat on his lower lip and he was growling. Her whole body shivered with sudden unexpected need, although now directed entirely toward him. She leaned close, ready for him to do whatever he wanted.

His nostrils flared and he gripped both her arms, still growling in a possessive way peculiar to vampires and shifters. The air seemed to swell and heat up, then suddenly Malik roared.

She only really figured things out when Malik released her abruptly and launched at Axton. She stepped back several feet until her back was against the vines. She grabbed onto a couple of thick stems and held tight because the fight was on.

Her own wraith fangs itched to descend as she watched the men rolling in the dirt, snarling, both sets of fangs exposed. Blood flew in all directions as one or the other would break skin.

Malik got in a solid punch to Axton's jaw, but he retaliated by rolling swiftly and throwing Malik into the air.

Axton then levitated and shoved his head into Malik's chest, which threw Malik against the stone monolith not far from Willow.

But Malik wasn't a mastyr vampire for nothing and he launched in Axton's direction, swept upward in the last second then caught Axton's head in a choke hold and squeezed hard.

Axton flipped around several times, finally wrenching himself from Malik's control, then lifted his palm where battle energy gathered. Malik did the same.

Two blue streams of electric heat and energy released and met in the middle. An enormous ball of white heat and fire rose from the center.

Both Axton and Malik began moving toward each other, the blue-and-white fire growing larger and hotter with each inch they covered.

And that's when Willow knew this would be a battle to the death, without either man surviving, if they sustained their battle frequencies. In the same way that she had an irrational drive toward both men, they would in turn fight on until a victor arose or they were both dead.

She left the vines and flew toward Evan, who now had a horrified look on his face. "Evan, you have to stop them. Use all the men. Split them up. Have them grab Malik and Axton at the same time from behind. Their touch will break the energy streams. You'll see."

"Got it."

She levitated and flew well away from the Guardsmen.

Evan coordinated his men and just as the ball of fire would have exploded, the Guardsmen caught each of the mastyrs around the waist and just like that, both mastyrs drew in their blast frequencies.

The air smelled burnt.

Axton fought against the hold the three Guardsmen had on him, while Malik, as soon as he recognized Evan's voice, dropped to the ground and sat down, breathing hard.

Willow ignored Axton and kept herself focused on Malik. He lifted his gaze to her and his voice, full of rage, pierced her mind, *You're not to look at other men.*

In any other circumstance, she would have yelled at him for such a chauvinistic attitude. But her own body was in an uproar, screaming for his attention, a result of the battle, of the way he looked at her, of the sight of his fangs still low on his lips, of his torn, bloody clothes.

The vein in her neck thrummed.

Sweet Goddess, she wanted him bad.

Evan shouted a few things at Axton, who shortly afterward took off. But her attention was all for Malik. With Axton out of the picture, she started moving toward him. He rose to his feet, his arms cut up, his eyes wild, his fangs an erotic invitation.

Evan must have understood, because he took the Guardsmen away.

Willow knew exactly what was going to happen, but she didn't want it to take place out in the open so she ran in the direction of the entrance to the colony. Just as she reached the vines, Malik was on her, turning her in his arms to face him, and trapping her in a caveman-like embrace.

Her body melted against his.

She pressed herself backward, however, taking him into the vines. He held her gaze, his nostrils working like bellows, his fangs fully extended. He made grunting noises that had her sex clenching hard.

She moved to the side, and with the vines behind her, she called to them to close up the entrance and give them privacy.

As Malik worked his zipper, she got her shoes off, then her jeans and her thong. He lifted her up and she slid her legs around his hips. Holding his cock in his hand, he found her entrance and began pushing inside. She was so wet and so ready and each thrust felt like heaven.

She angled her head, her heart laboring with the additional blood she'd created for him. Definitely a blood rose.

She whimpered as he licked up and down her throat, grunting again. She felt the sides of his fangs as he nuzzled her. *Malik, do it, please. I'm in agony.*

He didn't say anything or even attempt a telepathic communication. On some level, she knew he couldn't. He'd devolved into something that resembled what his species had looked and acted like tens of thousands of years ago.

And she loved it.

With her legs, she tightened her hold on his waist and kept him anchored as he drove his cock into her. He was a solid, hard missile, working her just right.

Then he struck, sinking his fangs to just the right depth so that her blood flowed into his mouth. Her whole body trembled with need and desire.

Malik smelled like battle as well, as though his rich forest scent had been lit on fire. The vines around her moved wildly, slapping erotically at her arms and legs and at him, then surrounding them both as they had earlier, binding them together.

Malik sucked heavily on her neck and with each pull, her inner well tugged on him. The earlier lovemaking had been almost tender, but this spoke to another side of her nature – blood rose or not – that loved being connected to the wilderness, the forest, all that was wild.

"Malik, you're fucking me." Had such words really left her mouth? Where was this boldness coming from?

He continued to grunt as he suckled, his hips moving faster now. She felt a vibration from him first at her throat where he drank from her, then between her legs as he revved up the frequency he could release through his cock.

She cried out at the dual sensations, grinding her hips against him, her body arching.

I'm so close.

Come for me, Willow. Come hard. And come now.

His deep resonant voice in her head, the vibrations of his stiff cock thrusting in and out, and the feel of his mouth holding her neck captive, pushed her straight over the cliff.

The orgasm ripped through her, opening her vocal chords wide. She screamed. The pleasure was so intense, more than she'd ever experienced before.

He let go of her neck, holding her gaze, his eyes boring into her as he continued to thrust heavily inside her. And just as she was easing back from the orgasm, he commanded, "Come for me again, Willow. Now."

His words were like magic, taking her over the precipice once more. Her neck arched, and pleasure stroked her deep as his cock hit her in just the right place. She screamed as an intense sensation rose into her abdomen, pleasure on pleasure, flowing through her chest, her heart, and straight up into her mind.

He moved faster now and lights exploded in her brain. She knew that she hadn't stopped screaming but she was also pretty sure she'd left the planet.

She heard him shouting and the feel of his release added to her own thrill. Her mind whirled and eddied, streaking through a vast sea of stars.

When she finally returned to herself, she had her arms draped over Malik's shoulders and he was breathing hard, petting her hair all the way down her back. The vines clung to her and to him, another layer of perfect sensation.

"I think you should get Axton back here, because that was incredible."

She'd meant it as a joke, but Malik drew back and pierced her gaze with his own. "Don't even speak that bastard's name." He then kissed her, forcing her against the wall of vines once more, penetrating her mouth in a way that had her panting all over again.

This time, when he pulled away, he asked in a harsh voice, "Have you got it, Willow? You're mine."

She put her hand on his face. "Then I suggest you stick close, Mastyr, because this is an unbonded blood rose thing, and I don't exactly have control over my response to other mastyrs. Have *you* got that?" Boldness again.

He growled, though more softly than before, and slid his arms all the way around her. "Sweet Goddess, I want to take you again. And again."

Shivers chased down her shoulders and back. "Oh, Malik. This was incredible and the moment I saw your fangs, even before you battled Axton, I needed you, had to have you."

He blinked and shook his head and she could tell he was coming back to himself. "Damn, I was so out of control." He narrowed his gaze at her. "I didn't hurt you, did I?"

"Not even a little.

He drew a deep breath and pushed her hair behind her shoulder, then kissed her throat. "Thank you for sharing with me again. I still can't believe how much better I feel. Thank you."

She held his gaze for a long moment. He was still inside her, still connected and it felt wonderful. She really didn't want the moment to end, so she made no effort to encourage him to disengage. "I guess we're going to have to work together, aren't we?"

He rubbed her arms and her lower back as though he, too, wanted to stay right where they were. "I think so, because I'll be damned before I ever let Axton get close to you again."

She slid her hand beneath his shirt and fondled his neck. "And I don't want him near me. I loathed the blood rose part of me that responded to him."

"If it's any consolation, I knew exactly what had happened, and that you would never willingly choose that man."

"This part is really upsetting to me."

"I know. Me, too. I can't remember the last time I brawled with another vampire." He glanced at the cuts on his arms and his torn shirt. He then sighed heavily and met her gaze once more. "I know I should move things along, but I hate the thought of separating from you right now."

"I feel the same way."

He kissed her, a long lingering kiss, sliding his arms around her again and pulling her close. She'd been so long without a man in her life that she'd forgotten how wonderful these moments could be.

After he slowly withdrew from her body, he reached down and tore a fairly clean portion of his shirt apart, handing her the remnant. "Thought this might help."

Her cheeks grew warm again as she tucked the cloth between her legs. She'd forgotten this part as well, that when a man left his seed behind, it wasn't always a simple matter to get on with things.

She quickly donned her thong and her jeans, socks and shoes.

He was looking around at the vines, when she was finally ready to face him. "So, we're in the middle of the entrance to the protected part of your property."

"Yes," she said. "This is a very short tunnel through the granite monolith." Once more, she debated how much she should tell him about the wraith colony, but decided he should just see everything for himself. "Malik, I think it might be best if you got to know these families before you made a final decision about relocation."

"I'd like that, but you should know that I'm set on this course."

"I understand, which is why I really want you to meet all of them. But first, I need you to take me back to my treehouse because we both need to get cleaned up. You have blood on your arms and on your uniform, for one thing. And I'll want to wear something very different from my jeans."

~ ~ ~

As Malik flew Willow back to her treehouse, his mind began to clear. The powerful, animal-like drive he'd experienced that had caused him to battle Axton, had also sent a strange, sludge-like hormone through his veins.

When he'd left the vine-laden entrance with her, he'd half-expected to be dragging his fists on the ground. Fortunately, he seemed to have come back to himself.

Once he arrived at her bedroom treehouse, he took stock of his Guardsman coat and shirt, as well as the blood on his skin and a few painful lacerations that he needed to heal. Just scrubbing up in the bathroom was not going to make him very presentable.

As he watched her pull a long, light green silk dress from the cupboard, his eyes widened. "You're going to wear that?"

Willow laid the gown out on the bed. "One of the couples will receive us formally."

Though it wasn't a full-out ball gown, it was the type of dress the fae often wore during ceremonies. He hardly knew what to make of this except that he now had a strong suspicion that the families Willow protected weren't your average wraiths. "We aren't talking about a couple of farmers and their families, are we?"

She shrugged. "Two or three of them work the land, but otherwise, no."

He moved closer. "Willow, what the fuck is going on here?"

She glanced up at him. "I'm breaking a big rule by taking you to see these people, but I swear I don't want to say more than that. I just need you to see and to judge this for yourself."

He stared at her for a long moment. He could have demanded more information, but something in her serious demeanor told him to go with the flow. "All right, that's fine. I get it; your restraint comes from your commitment to protect these families."

"That's exactly right."

"There's only one problem."

"What's that?" She actually looked confused.

He held up the torn sleeve of his shirt, then displayed the rip down the side of his Guardsman coat as well as the deep lacerations on his arm only partially healed.

She frowned slightly and he swore she'd never looked prettier, even though she, too, was smudged with battle stains because of what they'd done in the vines. "That is a problem."

"I'm going to head home, get cleaned up, healed up and I'll be back within the hour. How does that sound?"

Her shoulders relaxed. "I think that's the best idea yet."

Once the decision was made, he kissed Willow then took off out the door of the bedroom treehouse, launching high into the air above the forest canopy.

He flew slowly at first, until he realized that the more time he spent apart from Willow the greater the chance another mastyr could swoop in.

He put on some speed.

He'd never showered so fast in his life and didn't give a damn that some of his cuts weren't healed or that the soap hurt like a bitch.

As he dried off, he worked at his healing and fell over once just trying to get into a fresh pair of leathers. He felt desperate to return to Willow and make sure she was safe.

By the time he was back in the air, he contacted her. *Everything okay?*

Yes, fine. But are you okay? You sound out of breath.

He could tell by her tone that she was a little bewildered by his concern, which meant everything at her treehouse was just fine. *I'm good. I'll be there right away.*

He ate up the miles, flying faster than he ever had, so that in less than two minutes he touched down on her porch and knocked on her door.

"Come in. I'm almost ready."

But when he opened the door, he almost fell over again. Willow had no doubt showered and now looked dressed for a party. She'd pulled part of her hair up on top of her head, the rest dangling down her back. She wore the dress he'd seen laid out on the bed, the front cut low so that he had an excellent view of a perfect line of cleavage. She'd donned a necklace made up of a string of quarter-inch amethyst crystals which set off her creamy skin and auburn hair. The gown touched the tops of flat gold sandals with a string of small amethysts on the front cross-straps.

"You look … amazing."

She touched the sides of the gown. "Thank you."

"And very much on the formal side. I'm feeling underdressed."

At that, she came to him and placed her hand on the padded shoulder of his coat. "You look perfect. Your Guard uniform is revered among these … families."

And there it was again. He was sure she was holding back, telling him just enough so that she wasn't quite lying to him. "If you're ready, then let's go."

She nodded. "I'm ready."

He returned to the porch and the next moment she stood on his boot and he was holding her tight around her waist.

Before he took off, however, he kissed her, which made her sigh in response.

When he drew back, he looked at her for a long moment. "Willow, I don't know what all this means, but you're important to me. I want you to know that."

She nodded. "I know. And you're important to me."

She then tucked in her gown and leaned her head against his shoulder, holding him tighter still.

He levitated above the canopy again and headed back to the granite monolith, the fall of vines, and the secret entrance to the place where the wraiths lived.

"I take it we're expected," he said, as he touched down and she stepped off his boot.

"Yes, of course. I contacted one of the leaders, so we'll be welcomed formally as I thought we would be. But I should warn you that there will be a small ceremony of greeting, then we'll be given a tour. But first I want to assure you that what you're about to see was never meant as a reflection of your rule as Mastyr of Ashleaf, but of the need for these pure blood wraiths to protect themselves. Please remember that."

"Now you have me shaking in my boots."

But that made her laugh. She then waved her arm and at least half the vines simply vanished. She led him inside and once the vines behind them returned, she again waved her arm and the rest disappeared.

He blinked and, for a moment, had to shield his eyes because all he saw was a strong white light. The vampire in him interpreted the glow as something dangerous and he kept his boots planted to the ground inside what proved to be a short tunnel cut through the monolith.

She turned back to him and extended her hand. "The light is created by the people. You'll see. It's very safe for both fae and vampires."

He took her hand and by now he'd gotten used to the glow and knew that it wasn't at all like the damaging rays of the sun. But how the hell was it possible for wraiths to create this kind of illumination?

As the remaining vines moved out of Willow's way, and together they stepped into the light, what greeted his eyes caused him to stop dead in his tracks.

"What the hell?" he murmured beneath his breath. *What is this, Willow? What am I looking at and how could I not have known this existed in my realm?*

She turned to him. "I never wanted to lie to you, Malik, but I withheld the knowledge of this very ancient wraith colony because I'm their Protector."

He stood beside her and let his gaze travel slowly around what was a large town square, the street laid with granite pavers, shops on both sides over which families lived. Every window and doorway was jammed with wraiths watching them, and the square was full of curious citizens as well. But what also surprised him was that most of these wraiths were in what he believed was a fae form.

He turned to Willow. "Fae, yet not fae?"

"It's the form these wraiths can take to move more easily about in the world. The shifting from fae to wraith is a skill that is learned from childhood."

He shook his head because his mind spun. He couldn't seem to make sense of what he was looking at.

She once again took his hand. "Come this way. I want you to meet the leaders of this colony, both of whom knew Davido a couple thousand years ago."

Sweet Goddess. Very few realm-folk lived into the range of multiple millennia.

The crowd that had gathered in the square, near a tall stone obelisk, parted for them until he saw a beautiful fae wearing an elaborate necklace of feathers and beside her an elegant male fae with his wavy hair swept away from his face. They were a handsome couple.

The closer he drew, however, the more he felt their shared power, a joint power that seemed to emanate from the earth. He understood in that moment that he was looking at Realm royalty, figures from past eons that had served the Nine Realms in a quiet capacity all their lives. He resonated with their commitment, just as he knew Willow did.

"Mastyr Malik, may I present Illiandra and Gervassay of the Ashleaf Realm Colony?" She turned to the couple. "Mistress Illiandra and Lord Gervassay, Vampire Mastyr Malik of Ashleaf Realm, in service these two-hundred-years."

Very formal.

Illiandra spoke. "We are honored to meet you at last, Mastyr Malik. My husband and I welcome you to our colony and we've opened our hearts and our homes to you this fine realm night. Mistress Willow, will you and Mastyr Malik receive a blessing?"

"We will."

Malik felt the pressure of Willow's hand on the inside of his arm and didn't at first know what she meant by it, until two lovely young fae girls moved forward to spread out a thick rug before the couple.

Willow leaned close and whispered, "We're expected to kneel." In any other circumstance, he might have balked at the requirement. He didn't expect anyone to ever abase themselves before him, all realm-folk being equal.

But right now, in Ashleaf Colony, a frequency rose up and surrounded him of such great peace, that he felt as though he must be in the presence of the Goddess. Maybe he was.

He lowered himself to his knees and Willow followed suit. He bowed his head, so overcome that his soul felt ready to bust out of his skin.

As Illiandra began speaking in a different language, every vibration he possessed moved softly through his body. His surroundings were completely forgotten as the woman's voice rose and fell. In the middle of it, he took Willow's hand and she gave his fingers an answering squeeze. He could feel that she was as overwhelmed as he was.

Odd to think he'd expected to meet a few wraith families living in various farmhouses, and instead he found a large town and a spiritual depth that stunned him.

When Illiandra finished, he felt her touch his shoulder, the cue to rise. The moment he gained his feet, Willow as well, the two girls quickly gathered up the rug.

For a long moment, Malik could neither move nor speak. His heart felt incredibly full. He finally turned in a slow circle, wanting to greet all the onlookers as well, the very quiet fae-wraiths that watched him with open, innocent expressions. How different they were from the Invictus, those wraiths turned by Margetta's foul methods into vicious killers.

He lifted his arms, palms up, then spoke in a loud voice. "I am so happy to meet all of you tonight." He then pressed one fist against his chest.

There was silence for a moment, after which a loud sustained cheering filled the square.

He turned with a question in his eyes toward Willow, but she only smiled. *They love you,* she pathed. *They know the sacrifices you've made, the laws you've instituted on their behalf. Many of them have half-breed children, and grand-children in various parts of the Nine Realms.*

Malik had never needed to be told his role was valuable in Ashleaf. Hell, one of the first things he'd done was to enact laws to protect wraiths and half-breeds. But this acknowledgement, so full of obvious appreciation and gratitude, moved him as nothing else could.

He took another turn and waved, meeting as many pairs of eyes as he could. He nodded and smiled, and from his heart silently thanked these fellow realm-folk who'd lived in constant danger from Axton and The Society all these centuries.

At last, he faced Illiandra and Gervassay again, and the latter lifted his arms, encouraging the crowd to quiet down. "And now, Illiandra and I will show Mastyr Malik our fair town."

This seemed to be a prearranged cue, because the town folk scattered like mad, running here and there back to their shops and dwellings. Many laughing collisions couldn't be avoided.

Malik had no idea what was going on until the wraith couple took the lead, asking Malik and Willow to follow behind.

Okay, he never thought he'd be part of a processional going down what proved to be two miles of a very long High Street. It turned out that the few wraith families Willow protected was a township with surrounding farms, villages and hamlets for a combined population some twenty thousand strong.

He'd never smiled so much or felt so deeply honored in his entire existence than during this walk he shared with Willow. Many called out her name as well and blessed her for her service. She blushed often, as if unused to the accolades.

At the end of the High Street, a small villa came into view. But what caught his eye was how the land really opened up, and he had to blink several times. Ashleaf Realm as a forested mountain world had little pasture and farmland, yet that's exactly what he saw as a soft, green landscape rolled to the western horizon as far as the eye could see.

And Willow's protective spell had kept all of this from view.

He tried to think just how many times he might have flown over the same square miles – thousands of times, no doubt – but he had no real recollection of any unaccounted for land.

Once more he was stunned by Willow's level of power and how she could prevent even his eyes from seeing this land.

When Illiandra reached the path to the villa, she turned to him. "Gervassay and I would like Willow to show you the breadth of the colony, if you would fly her over. And when you're done, come back here and we'll share a meal together. How does that sound?"

"Wonderful." Yet, the word seemed inadequate.

Gervassay offered his arm to his wife, and when they headed down the front path to their home, Malik took Willow high into the air so he could get a bird's eye view of the protected twenty square miles. To Willow, he pathed, *How do you do it? How do you shield this much land?*

He passed over a number of farms and a few smaller villages and hamlets. The countryside was more pastoral than any other part of his realm.

I'll make a confession, Willow responded. *One of the reasons I decided to bring you here was because I've reached some sort of limit in my protective ability.*

Alexandra the Bad taught me well and I've gained in power under Illiandra's tutelage. But right now, I'm maxed out. If one more baby is born, or one more home built, or if any of the flocks increase in size, I don't think I'll be able to offer the same level of protection.

You've been burdened.

I'm not complaining, Malik, I promise you that. I've loved serving the colony all this time. It's been my privilege.

He thought about the deaths of her parents. *And a way of honoring your mother's family.*

Yes, at the very least that.

But now you need help.

There's no question in my mind that I can't do this alone anymore.

Chapter Five

Later, Willow sat beside Malik at Illiandra's table. Their hostess served a simple vegetable soup with stoneware in a beautiful shade of dark teal. Slices of flavorful herbed goat cheese, toasted sour dough bread with a hint of basil-butter, and home-grown tomato slices tasted of heaven.

The flight with Malik had shifted something inside Willow that she found very hard to define. He was no longer just the mastyr of the realm or the man who had chased her through the forest. With each shared encounter, he was becoming more real, more man, more of a companion and that scared her. And he was the only realm-person, besides Illiandra, who knew that she'd reached the limits of her ability to properly guard the colony.

She'd never thought she'd end up with a vampire one day. Her desire had always tended to more intellectual fae males, and her fantasies had involved being married, having babies, and living close to one of the Realm universities.

Mating with a vampire had never entered her thoughts. Of course she was drawn to Malik and in one sense how could she be anything else? He was handsome with large brown eyes that right now had fixed themselves on Gervassay as the fae spoke, of all things, about septic tanks. Of course, waste management in a mountainous realm like Ashleaf was a serious topic.

She was tuned into Malik, the level of his interest in the colony, his enjoyment of the savory soup, and his constant concern for the inhabitants of Ashleaf, including pure-blood wraiths.

Once the septic tank issue had been fully explored, Illiandra asked, "I heard a report that you're talking about relocating all the half-breeds in Ashleaf to Swanicott Island."

Malik didn't even flinch as he met Illiandra's gaze. "I have no choice. The recent murders, which I'm sure you know about, have made the decision for me. I won't have another half-breed's death on my conscience. And by the same token, given Axton's intention to breach the hidden entrance, I think we should talk about relocating your colony as well."

Willow dropped her spoon, clattering it on her bread plate. She turned to Malik. "You're bringing that up now?"

He met her gaze, then looked away, his eyes growing pained. He shook his head several times. "I don't see why not." He glanced from Gervassay to Illiandra. "Maybe you've lived a safe, cloistered existence, but since The Society took over, I've had over three hundred murders to contend with. And I won't have one more." He lifted both hands, as though the matter was settled.

Both Illiandra and Gervassay appeared somber, but hadn't reacted as Willow had expected. Something else seemed to be on their minds.

Gervassay folded his hands in his lap. "There's just one problem."

"And what's that?" Malik's deep voice, full of tension, sounded loud in the small dining area.

"Our people won't leave. Haven't you guessed it, yet Malik? Felt it? I believe you must have when my wife blessed the two of you in the town square."

Malik, his jaw bearing a stubborn line, once more shook his head. "The blessing was absolutely beautiful, no question. But beyond that—"

Illiandra spoke quickly. "Malik, what my husband is not saying is that there's something else you need to understand and perhaps experience. Let me ask you this, can you feel a vibration beneath you, coming from the earth?"

"I can," Willow offered. "I feel it all the time when I'm here in the colony or anywhere on my land."

Malik glanced at her, his brow pinched. "Yes, of course I feel it. It's like a humming. Is this where the light comes from as well?"

Illiandra nodded. "Absolutely. What you're feeling is the heartbeat of the Nine Realms. This is where it all began, the birthplace of our world, and where the Goddess, our Creator, set everything in motion."

Willow had never heard Illiandra speak of the Ashleaf Colony in that way before, but she felt her words as truth. She also wanted to give expression to something she'd been considering for a long time. "We're all wraiths, aren't we? All of us in the Nine Realms?"

Malik looked at her as though she'd just gone insane, but Illiandra nodded. "We are. The wraith genome is the base from which all other species evolved. It's why we're compatible and can intermarry."

Malik stared at Illiandra for a long moment. His lips parted. "And you're sure of this?"

"One-hundred percent certain."

Malik narrowed his gaze. "It would explain so much that we come from a common root." He smiled, shook his head, then began to laugh.

"What is it?" Willow asked, overlaying his arm with her hand. "What's so funny?"

"I'm thinking about The Society and their mission to destroy all half-breeds, when essentially every realm-person is part wraith."

"That's exactly right." Illiandra stroked the feathers at her chest.

Malik's gaze fell to her fingers. "Huh. I thought that was a necklace, but it's … part of you, isn't it?"

"Yes, it is." Illiandra's turn to smile. "And now, I have a suggestion, because I think you've both been through a lot tonight." She rose as she spoke.

Willow glanced up at her, waiting expectantly.

Illiandra's smile broadened, "Why don't you take Malik to get some ice cream. We have some of the best here in the Nine Realms."

~ ~ ~

"Ice cream?" Malik was incredulous. He'd been talking about relocating an entire colony of wraiths to an island off the coast of Swanicott Realm, then learned that he was part wraith. And now, he and Willow should go get some ice cream?

He met Willow's gaze and saw the laughter dancing in her hazel eyes. "It sounds so *normal,* doesn't it? Something neither of us are used to?"

He considered her words and the light in her eyes, then felt something inside his chest finally relax. Maybe Illiandra had a point. "No, that we're not." He gained his feet and offered his hand. "But I'd love one piece of normal right now."

A few minutes later, he held Willow's hand as he walked her down the cobbled street. The town was very attractive with large baskets of flowers hanging from the lampposts. Many of the townsfolk waved from doorsteps and windows, but for the most part left them in peace.

He asked Willow about her nightly existence and how she spent her time. She was a fan of reading, especially essays on avocations like gardening and forest exploration. She enjoyed listening to classical music while crocheting or sometimes drawing.

"I lead a very quiet life as you can imagine."

"You've missed a lot."

"I suppose you could view it that way, and maybe I have, but I don't necessarily feel that way. Do you think your life has been lacking?"

Malik frowned slightly. "Good question, so the answer would have to be similar to yours: yes and no. I guess I don't think in those terms. Mostly, I want to fulfill my duties as mastyr to the best of my ability."

"And I want to protect the people here." She gestured to a group of children playing by a large fountain in the middle of the street. They weren't in any real danger – the colony having no cars, just bicycles and donkey-driven carts.

A couple of the children in wraith form, half-ran and half-flew in their direction. The older ones did a couple of intricate loops in the air. The wraith form was somewhat elongated and very lightweight compared to the sturdier fae or other realm-folk physiques.

The oldest girl landed on her feet, not as a wraith but as a fae. "Very neat trick," he called out.

She beamed, showing the loss of two front teeth. "Thank you, Mastyr. So, are you going to marry Willow? We hope you do. We all love her."

She grabbed Willow's hand, and he saw the blush that climbed Willow's cheeks.

You're beloved here, he pathed.

And I love this community.

A young boy wraith, struggling to hold himself steady in the air, looked at Malik. "Will you give us a toss?"

Malik smiled. "Where's your mother?"

The boy gestured with a jerk of his chin. Malik turned toward the adult in question, "Will you allow it, Mistress?"

The woman, in her fae form, nodded. "He's old enough, but thank you for asking."

Malik picked the boy up and with a one-two-three, tossed him high in the air.

The boy squealed as he did a few flips then drifted into a careful flight to the ground. "Again?"

Of course the sight of one boy having fun, brought children clustering around his knees. He had only one recourse and repeated the process over and over, always checking with the nearby parent. More than one toddler got led away crying because mama refused.

He spent the next half hour tossing child after child into the air and watching the delicate loops each could make while in their wraith form.

Malik hadn't enjoyed himself this much in a long time. He rarely stopped in any of the villages to talk or play with the children.

Eventually, he called a halt and continued to the ice cream shop, ordering lemon for Willow and toffee for himself. He sat with her outside on a bench in one of at least a dozen narrow grassy belts that ran down the center of the street.

Many wraiths, usually in fae form and a few actually sporting feathers like Illiandra, came by and thanked him for his service and for his support of half-breeds in Ashleaf.

A small wraith toddler, levitating while holding onto the bench and anything else she could reach, finally found Malik and held her arms up to him. He glanced at her mother who nodded her acquiescence.

He lifted the light-as-a-feather girl and she promptly relaxed against him leaning her head into the crook of Malik's neck. He continued chatting with Willow about the various wraith villages he'd spotted from the air in between licking his cone and holding the child.

When Willow fell silent, he asked, "Is something wrong?"

"No, not at all, but are you aware that the baby has fallen asleep on your shoulder?"

"Oh, I guess she has."

"Malik, have you ever had kids?"

"No."

"You must be a natural, then."

"I don't know about that, but I like them."

She smiled. "Do you want children, lots of vampire toddlers running around your villa?"

"I guess I'd always thought one day, maybe. I don't know." But when he looked into the future, all he saw was more of The Society and Axton and now he had a colony to worry about.

Willow touched his knee. "Hey, I didn't mean to distress you."

He spoke quietly. "I just honestly don't know what to do about all these families. If they choose to remain and Axton is after them, it's only a matter of time before he breaks through."

"Well, I suppose that will resolve itself soon enough, but right now, I'm thinking you look very sexy holding that child over your shoulder." She settled her hand on his arm.

Malik's gaze shot to hers and he didn't mistake the look in her eye. That her sweet forest-rain scent suddenly perfumed the air made him wish he had her alone.

"Sexy, huh?"

She nodded.

"Well, I've got another arm. I could probably hold a couple more, if only to keep seeing that look on your face."

~ ~ ~

Willow chuckled softly, but she hadn't been kidding. Watching him so at ease with the wraith children had lit her up like crazy. She was very female and, yes, she found herself longing for a family of her own especially when she happened to see mothers with their children.

She gave herself a shake, however, refusing to start wishing for things that couldn't be, at least not right now when she had twenty-thousand souls to tend to.

But perhaps what moved her about Malik was that he loved and cared for his realm in the same way he held this little girl.

She liked this man a lot, even if he was a warrior.

Just as she opened her mouth to tell him as much, a familiar dizziness overcame her as well as an acute awareness that a new charm now worked against her protective vine shield.

So soon? She couldn't believe it. Whoever the fae was that had been creating these spells, she had tremendous power, more than Willow had ever experienced before.

"Malik," she said quietly. "Trouble."

He frowned. "As in serious?"

"Another charm, and much more powerful than the last. The whole colony is in danger. I need to let Illiandra know. She'll sound the alarm."

He nodded, then rose and searched for the mother of the wraith-child. She wasn't far, just chatting with another woman also holding a sleeping child. When he inclined his head to her, the woman hurried to him and drew her baby into her arms.

Willow pathed to Illiandra, alerting her to the new danger. A moment later, the white light that filled the town began to dim in slow stages and a soft whistling passed down the high street. Willow had seen practice drills, and this one went exactly as expected.

Every citizen simply melted into the surrounding streets and homes. When the light disappeared entirely, the town was in complete black-out, the stars above the only illumination.

Willow felt a strange vibration above her and looking up she saw smoke forging a hole in her protective shield. She rose to her feet and focused all her energy on her shield, but the spell was like a constant battering against her stream of energy, becoming more powerful as each second passed.

At the same time, she sensed a warning from the protective spell around her treehouse complex. "Malik, someone is in my home going through my things. This isn't good. If it's a fae, the one making these charms, she'll be collecting articles that she'll use to cast a spell against me."

He took his cell from his leathers. "I'll get some Guardsmen over there right now. Is the spell at your gate still down?"

Willow nodded, but she trembled. The energy she streamed pulsed through her, causing her to break out in a sweat. Her hands shook.

He shifted away from her then spoke quietly into his phone. After a moment, he addressed her. "Evan is sending a squad over to your main treehouse right now."

"Thank you." She'd been so right to involve Malik.

As she continued to focus her energy on holding the protective shield, she could sense that Axton's spell had dual parts. He was not only attacking the shield as a whole, but he was also burning the vines at the entrance.

There was one thing, however, that didn't make sense. "Wasn't Evan at the entrance to the colony when you spoke to him? Near the vines?"

"Yes, he was."

"Well, didn't he see Axton? I can feel that he's right there."

Malik shook his head. "He reported that nothing was going on."

"Call him again."

Malik immediately got Evan on the phone. "Hey, Willow insists that we've got a spell burning the entrance vines and Axton is right next to them."

Her legs shook now with the effort to sustain the shield, and she felt lightheaded.

She watched Malik listening hard. He then covered the phone with his other hand and said quietly, "Evan says that the vine looks the same to him, green and healthy."

"Great. Axton is hidden behind a shield." Could this get any worse?

Malik relayed the information to Evan, afterward returning the cell to his pocket.

Sweat dripped down her back and between her breasts with the effort to keep repairing both the shield above her and the vines at the entrance. "I won't be able to hold this much longer."

"Willow, how do we break the spell?"

"The same way as last time. We need to physically stop Axton, find the charm and smash it."

"Then I'll get over to the entrance."

Willow shook her head. "I don't think we should be separated, Malik, not right now and that's my fae instinct talking. We've been brought together for a reason."

"You're right. So how about you focus all your energy on Axton."

"I can't. If I let go of the protective shield for a second either Axton will breach the entrance or this hole above me will explode and the entire shield will collapse." Her arms shook. "Malik, I'm frightened. I'm so close to losing control here."

Malik frowned. "You're shaking."

"Yes, I am."

Malik grabbed her arms and the moment he touched her, power flared within her body and a new, second stream of energy began to flow straight from the heart of the realm as though it recognized him.

He glanced down at his feet. "Holy shit, that's coming from the earth."

"I know. I can feel it as well. Just keeping holding my arms."
She channeled all that power into her protective shield and lifting
her gaze, she watched the hole seal up in a sudden quick wave.

Closing her eyes, she turned her attention to the entrance
vines and visualized them reforming and repulsing the charm.
Power moved in heavy waves straight to the entrance.

A moment later, the sound of an explosion rolled through
the colony. She was running before she knew what she was doing,
heading to the vines on the colony side of the monolith. Malik was
right on her heels.

When she reached the vines, she waved them aside in stages,
though the familiar burned smell filled the tunnel.

With the last lift of her hand, the damaged vines disappeared
and she passed through to the other side, but Axton wasn't there.
The ground, however, looked scorched and a couple of Malik's
Guardsmen were patting their smoking shirts.

Malik called to Evan. "What happened out here?"

The levitating Guardsmen touched down.

Evan waved an arm in the direction of the vines. "A kind of
explosion, but it happened so fast, I couldn't even tell you what hit
us. Energy exploded outward through this area where the vines are
and that's when I saw Axton where you said he was. But he took off
before I could engage."

"Is everyone okay?"

The four remaining Guardsmen nodded, and with that,
Willow released a deep sigh. "Thank the Goddess, because I think
it was my, or rather our joined power, that created the explosion."

"How?" Evan asked.

The question was so simple, but posed with such incredulity,
that Willow laughed. "I don't think either of us knows how we did

it. Although, the energy source seemed to come from the earth itself."

"Well those wraiths must be special to have brought you two together with so much ability, however strange it is."

Willow laughed again, then tears bit her eyes." She turned to Malik, and he seemed to understand because he drew her against him, wrapping her up in his arms.

"It's all over," he said against her cheek, holding her close.

"I'm not used to this," she whispered. "I'm not a warrior like you."

"I know."

She rested her head on his shoulder. "Axton will be back. You know he will."

"I have no doubt of that." He shifted slightly while still holding her so that Willow had a view of Evan. "I want a couple more squads out here just in case. I realize you couldn't do anything this time, but we might need you when he attacks again."

"Why the hell is Axton so intent on getting to these wraith families? He seems completely obsessed."

Willow felt certain it would be a mistake to reveal the whole truth about the colony, at least for now. *Malik, we can't tell him. Going public needs to come from the colony Elders.*

Malik nodded in agreement, then addressed Evan. "I think Axton has been on a mission from the time I took over as mastyr of this realm. He wants Ashleaf back and he wants to kill wraiths and half-breeds to get to that goal. I don't know how he learned that Willow has been protecting wraiths, but I have no doubt that once inside, he'll not only murder these families, he'll use their existence as a vehicle to poison more of our citizens against my rule."

Evan nodded. "You're right. That's exactly what he would do. Bastard."

"So, what's the word on Willow's home?"

"Ransacked. I'm sorry, Mistress. But by the time my squad got over there, the deed was done. I have several of my men standing guard."

"Thank you." She compressed her lips, biting back the tears. Her home had been her sanctuary during her long service as the Protector. And now someone had been inside doing a lot of damage.

"I'll be staying with Willow through the rest of the night as well as the day. You can reach me through my cell or path me if you need to. But I have a feeling that whatever Axton plans next, Willow will know about it first. Also, I want the Troll Brigade to stand watch from dawn until full-dark."

Evan got on his phone and made the calls. Within a few minutes, vampires began flying in.

Evan slid his phone back into the pocket of his leathers. "We're all set."

"Good. I'm going to take Willow home." He glanced up. "We've got a couple hours before dawn. And, if Axton doesn't make another play during that time, we should have some peace for the next twelve hours."

With those words, Willow began to relax. She pathed with Illiandra giving her an update and letting her know that she and Malik would be returning to her treehouse. Illiandra wished her good health and fruitful dreams and with that, Willow drew her night to a close.

The shield held, stronger than ever, but she was done in.

~ ~ ~

With Willow in his arms, Malik flew her back to her treehouse complex. But even he was stunned by what he saw. Windows had been smashed and an axe taken to the beautiful front walkway railing as well as the front door. Inside the house, the furniture had been destroyed.

This was an act of hatred.

He'd seen it before and it had one purpose: to create fear and chaos. Axton's hand was all over this.

Willow moved slowly and started to cross the room, but he caught her hand, holding her back. "I'm going to take care of this, but I want you to stick close to me. I don't want you hurt because something falls on you."

She nodded. Her skin was pale and her eyes painfully wide. She was clearly shocked out.

Still holding her hand, he got on his phone and contacted one of his favorite troll contractors and explained the situation.

Hank spoke the words Malik wanted to hear. "That fucking asshole is at it again. Okay, give me the coordinates and Mastyr, I will have both my teams at this residence within the hour."

When he delivered the basic realm map coordinates, Hank said, "Wait a minute, you're at Willow's property. Are you telling me that bastard wrecked Willow's home?"

Malik frowned. He knew that Willow kept a spell over her property. If a fae had done this, then she had tremendous power to have broken through the charm. "Not Axton. Someone aligned with him, though, and very powerful. I'm thinking one of the fae who sell on the black market."

"Well, fuck! I did the original work on that complex." A string of curses followed that made Malik smile.

Hank let him know about when he would arrive, then hung up.

Malik squeezed Willow's hand. "Hank is coming."

"Hank, the contractor?" Tears filled her eyes and the next moment, she was hugging him hard and pathing, *Thank you, thank you, thank you.*

"Hey, it's what I do."

She laughed at that, then lifted her face to him. "I mean it. Thank you. This was the worst ending to a long, difficult night and you've made it better, almost tolerable." She then pulled away from him and looked around. Every wall had been damaged. "Hank will be furious."

"Yeah, he already is. I don't suppose you have beer in the house, do you?"

"Oh, what a good idea."

She started to cross the kitchen area, but again he held her back. "Let me go first, just in case."

He moved quickly into the kitchen and tested the support branch, but it held. He moved inside and opened the fridge. Sitting there, lined up in perfect waiting order, were several cold bottles of brew.

He smiled. He loved this woman.

He loved this woman.

He'd meant it only as a flippant response to Willow keeping beer in her fridge, but the words kept sinking deeper and deeper. And as he turned toward her, with her green silk dress still unmolested by recent events, his heart stopped all over again.

Was this love he felt or the beginning of love?

And had she always been this beautiful with her creamy skin and thick wavy auburn hair, her hazel eyes and softly arched brows? Or was it her blood rose gift that made his heart swell, then squeeze up tight?

Right now, he didn't care. He let his gaze rest on her and savor what the Goddess had made so incredibly well. As he twisted the caps off and tossed them in a nearby wastebasket, he handed a beer to her.

She made no apologies as she drank deep.

He joined her.

Fucking Society that acted however it wanted to act. Somehow, if it was the last thing he did, he'd run it to ground. Maybe all that had happened in the past twenty-four hours had occurred to show him one simple thing: that Axton had the support of a fae powerful enough to destroy Willow's shield. And if Malik hadn't been there, the charm would have won the day.

What would have happened to the wraiths then?

And who was this fae that seemed to be in league with Axton? He knew that the black market was alive and well and that there were several very powerful, hidden fae in his realm that supplied charms for a price. But this one had to have Guild level powers.

The thought ran through his head that maybe Margetta the Ancient Fae, the one that had created the Invictus, might be involved. Yet he couldn't imagine Axton aligning himself with someone who was part wraith. And if she was involved, why wasn't his land filled with her army of wraith-pairs? For both those reasons, he tended to think Axton had made an alliance with a black market fae.

For now, at least, with dawn creeping closer, he could let it all go. Axton, as a vampire, wouldn't be active during the day.

He ran his hand over his night-old beard. He had one more call to make. He reached his housekeeper and gave her a list of things he needed, including something to sleep in and a fresh uniform for the next night. At the last minute, he requested jeans and a tee, since he'd be up for a while before he actually went to work at full-dark.

When he hung up, Willow touched his arm. "I'm glad you're staying here."

"I wouldn't be at ease anywhere else."

She glanced around, then drew a deep, bracing breath. "I want to see the rest of my complex."

"Okay, but let me lead the way."

"Happily."

Malik half expected to see the rope bridges sliced up so that Willow wouldn't be able to easily reach her different houses. Instead, it looked like the worst of the damage was in the main house and for that he was grateful.

But someone had gone through and ransacked each room, hunting for things, maybe, as Willow had suggested earlier, to use in spells against her.

"Let me know if you see anything missing."

"My brush," she said, moving into her bathroom. "My brush is gone and it has my hair in it."

Malik frowned. "As I recall, some of my hair was in there, too."

"That's not good. A lot can be done with hair in the creating of spells with an evil taint."

Malik saw the drawn look to her cheeks, and he crossed to her. "Listen, you're exhausted, and now isn't the time to try to deal with any of this."

"You're right."

"How about we head to your meditation porch and finish our beers? Once Hank and his team arrive, I'll have them go to work on the bedroom first, then we can both retire. The only problem is all the noise."

When she crossed the rope bridge to her meditation treehouse, she glanced at him and smiled. "Do you know that is one thing I can take care of? I don't do a lot of spell casting but working as I do, especially when I really need to sleep, sometimes the day-birds keep me awake. So, I devised my own noise-shield."

"Perfect."

Willow sat down in one of two chairs on a small porch that overlooked the forest.

He sat down beside her and for a long time, neither spoke. He finished his beer, then fetched two more for them. She took her second one readily, and once more he took up his place beside her and swigged.

The night sky studded with stars could be seen through the forest canopy, although with his vampire vision he saw everything as in a glow. Realm night-birds fought for the best nesting sites and kept up a mad chatter.

When he finally heard Hank calling to him, he told Willow to stay put while he headed to the primary house. The troll, bless him, had brought two very large crews, one for clean-up, the other for repair.

Of course, Hank let a few more 'fucks' and 'Goddess be-damneds' fly before he finally set his repair crew to work.

Malik waited on the front porch of the main house for the delivery of his clothes and once those arrived, he brought them back to the meditation treehouse.

"Hank said the work in the bedroom would be done in half an hour." He settled the clothes-bag by the doorway, then took up his chair once more.

"I'm so grateful, because I'm dead tired. Of course, the buzz from the beer is forcing my eyelids to sink when they might not otherwise." She sipped again, afterward shifting toward him slightly. "Should we just jump in and complete the blood rose bond? I mean, we're in the middle of rough seas, so do we risk way too much by holding back?"

He was so surprised by the question that for a long moment all he could do was stare at her. For himself, bonding was out of the question. He'd avoided any kind of relationship because his Vampire Guard battled both the dreaded Invictus wraith-pairs and The Society. He needed to stay centered on his duties.

But he was curious about her reasoning. "Do you want to bond with me?"

"No, of course not. Wait. That sounded bad. I really like you Malik and the sex is amazing, but I have a job to do that requires every ounce of my strength."

"But it would appear I can help with that."

She chuckled softly. "Are you planning on attaching yourself to my hip, because if you're not physically touching me, I don't see how this could actually work."

"Well, I know one thing for sure; I'm not making a decision like that tonight."

She laughed again, a sound that dug deep between his ribs. He even liked the way she laughed.

As he continued swigging his beer, he thought about Axton's latest attack and a jolt of anxiety went through him. Axton had almost pierced the colony's protective shield and what if he'd gotten through? He had no idea whether Axton knew he was after an entire colony or just a few families, but if he'd penetrated the entrance, he would have discovered the truth.

What a public relations' nightmare the colony's existence would have become for Malik. A thousand complaints would have flown to the Sidhe Council, demanding his removal.

And there was one more element he needed to remember. Axton had his own Guard. He'd kept it well-concealed all these years, but Malik knew of its existence; he just didn't know how big it was or how far Axton would be willing to go to get at the wraiths.

He decided then and there he needed reinforcements.

"I'm thinking of calling Zane in to help."

"Mastyr of Swanicott Realm?"

"Yes, I think I'm going to need additional support over the next couple of nights. I don't like the way any of this is shaping up, and I don't want to be caught flat-footed if Axton should decide to bring in his not-so-secret Guard force that is loyal to him." At least fifty Guardsmen, aligning with Axton, had left the Vampire Guard when Malik became Mastyr of Ashleaf. And Malik had no reason to believe that the numbers hadn't grown over the past two centuries.

"Sounds like a plan." She'd spoken quietly, and as she leaned back in her chair, he could see that her eyes were almost shut.

He slid his phone from his leathers and made the realm-to-realm call.

"Malik, how the fuck are you doing?" Zane had one of the deepest voices of all the mastyrs.

"I've been battling an upstart asshole who wants to kill a bunch of innocent people. How are you?"

Zane chuckled. "Up to my ass, as usual. So, what's going on, because you sound like nine kinds of gremlin shit, my friend."

Malik smiled. Zane had always been able to make him laugh. He was about to relay the details, when Willow rose to her feet, gesturing to the doorway behind him. He turned and saw that Hank was smiling and jerking his head toward the bedroom treehouse. It looked like all was ready.

He nodded to them both, and Willow left with Hank, talking quietly to him.

Malik turned his attention back to Zane and for the next several minutes he told his fellow mastyr about the goings on in his realm, including the whole blood rose thing. The only detail he held back was the existence of an entire colony of wraiths and instead used Willow's ploy about protecting a few hidden families on her land.

"The thing is, I don't know what fae is helping Axton out, but her power level is pretty high. I'm thinking one of the black market fae. So, what I need is for this entire area on Willow's property to be reinforced at full-dark, near the entrance to where the families live."

"How about me and fifty of my best Guardsmen head your way?"

A wave of relief rolled through Malik's chest. He hadn't realized how tense he'd been. "That would be perfect. I'll get back to you just after full-dark to give you the details and location. Just do whatever you can to stay away from Willow. I almost killed Axton for talking to her."

"Got it, but damn that must have felt good, taking that bastard on."

"Used my fangs and took a couple of chunks out of his fucking arms."

Zane laughed. "I would have paid to watch."

Malik fell quiet.

"What?" That bass voice rolled through the connection.

"I've never been out of control like that before."

When Zane spoke, his voice sounded hushed. "Is it like what they all say? A drive like none other?"

"Yep."

"Well, shit."

"You said it."

"So you wish it hadn't come?" Zane asked.

Malik was all set to answer, but when he thought of what it had been like, just a few minutes ago, sharing a beer with Willow, well, the words got stuck in his throat. "It's just very unexpected and surprising. I'm still adjusting."

"Do you think you'll bond with her?"

"I don't know. Early days yet."

Malik grew tense all over again, however, at the thought of Zane anywhere near Willow over the next couple of nights. But he'd already made the call and now he'd just have to figure out how to keep the two of them apart.

"You can use the training center and rotate your men through my treehouse rec room."

Zane sighed. "That lounge of yours; I remember it well. And it overlooks a bathing pool."

Yeah, the men liked looking.

Though the horizon was still pitch black, a warning sensation, like a clanging bell deep in his skull, told Malik that dawn approached.

"I'm headed to bed now. Talk to you tomorrow."

"Later."

After picking up his clothes bag, he made quick tracks across the rope bridge to the upper treehouse. He really needed a shower.

The room looked as tidy as ever; he owed Hank one.

But as he crossed the threshold and watched Willow climb into bed, he realized he'd been assuming he'd be joining her. Yet the last thing he wanted to do was to put any kind of pressure on her. "Where would you like me to sleep?" he asked, his heart pounding in his chest. He really wanted to be with her right now.

She smiled sleepily, pulling the covers up to her chin. "Here, of course." She patted the space next to her. "I'm too distressed to have you farther away than an elbow-nudge."

He smiled. "Okay, then. I'll shower up."

He laid the bag over the chair across from the bed. Though he usually slept in the nude, he'd planned on wearing PJ bottoms for Willow's sake. They might have hooked up a couple of times, but he didn't want her to think he had expectations.

He took his time showering so that by the time he got into bed, she was asleep.

Once under a light quilt, and the shades drawn against even the smallest ray of sunlight, Malik lay on his pillow stunned that he was here.

In her sleep, Willow tossed her hand in his direction but after making contact, she moved close so that she was stretched out beside him. He lifted his arm, and the next thing he knew, she nestled her head in the dip of his shoulder. He held her close and once again his heart seemed to light on fire with his growing affection for the woman.

Yeah, he was honest enough with himself to know that he could get used to this, to having her in his life. He just couldn't figure out how the pieces could all fit together.

His chest felt tight yet full at the same time, and his veins flowed with something very warm.

~ ~ ~

Willow awoke slowly on her stomach, feeling slightly drugged. The hour was late and it wouldn't be long until full-dark, which meant she'd slept over eleven hours. Unbelievable.

But then the prior night had been one of the roughest of her life.

Malik lay on his side facing her, his brows drawn together, as though even in his sleep he worried about Ashleaf Realm.

She could relate. She'd had a few unnerving dreams about wraith children dying.

She turned and stretched out on her back, giving her body and brain time to catch up. She blinked several times, trying to clear away the lethargy.

She recalled now that she'd awakened more than once in Malik's arms and his presence in her bed had done more to ease her than she wanted to admit.

Glancing at him again, she realized she could get used to having a big male body in her bed. Desire rose suddenly. The need to be kissed and held by him, to make love with him, swept through her. She almost reached for him with the intention of waking him up, but she held back.

He needed his sleep as much as she did and her instincts told her that tonight might be even more difficult than the previous night. The fae acting behind Axton was working fast on his behalf. Who knew what the pair would throw at them as the evening marched on.

More than once, she wondered if Margetta might be the fae, the one who'd created the Invictus. Her bid to take over the Nine Realms wasn't over and her army was always looking for wraiths to subvert. What if she'd discovered the existence of the Ashleaf Colony and wanted the pure-bloods for her army of vile wraith-pairs?

When her brain finally cleared and her thoughts made sense, she rose quietly, showered, and dressed for the night in jeans and a purple, tank top. After all that she'd been through, she didn't really want to be in a gown or even in her favorite long skirt.

She padded barefoot across the rope bridge toward the main treehouse. The waning sunlight bothered her a little and would definitely blister Malik given his extreme vampire sensitivity to the sun. But her faeness wasn't quite as affected and the short distance made it tolerable.

Right now, however, she wished she had a spell that could counteract the effect for Malik's sake.

When she reached her living room, she almost wept with relief. Her home looked perfectly restored and a bowl of fresh fruit sat on the counter with a note propped up beside it.

She opened the folded paper, and her eyes blurred with tears. Hank basically said that a couple of minor things needed to be taken care of, but otherwise her home was good to go.

Her spell had blocked all the noise, and by the looks of the repairs, Hank's crew would have made a serious racket for hours on end.

She slid the bowl across the counter and started working on a wonderfully ripe pineapple. A nice fruit salad would be exactly what was needed. Perhaps some eggs. Maybe a frittata.

And coffee. Definitely, coffee.

She spent the next half hour pulling ingredients together, including cutting thick slices off a slab of bacon. She set the table for two.

The scene was so homey that a fluttering started in her stomach and kept ranging northward to her heart. Between having found herself several times cradled in Malik's arms during the night, and seeing a table set for two, the solitary nature of her existence rode down on her like a heavy, autumn rain.

She had to sit down for a moment. Not once had she ever regretted her decision to become the wraith colony's Protector. And she didn't even feel any regret right now.

But during this short time with Malik, she was left with deep longings she couldn't easily set aside.

Maybe she'd been flippant last night — a state induced by the fact that she'd imbibed almost two beers in a very short period of time — when she'd asked Malik to bond with her. But right now, she swore that if he suggested it, she'd say yes.

The bacon sizzling in the pan called to her, and she returned to flip the strips again. The frittata was almost done as well.

She thought about returning to the bedroom treehouse to wake Malik up, but right then he called out that he'd join her shortly. She loved the sound of his deep male voice in her home.

The evening twilight had disappeared and full-dark now covered the forest, but her flexible fae vision began adjusting so that the woods always looked as though bathed in a soft golden glow.

How she loved her home and her world.

The night-birds, peculiar to the Nine Realms, had begun chattering as well, streaking from branch to branch, diving down to the stream to drink and to bathe. From the kitchen window, she could see down into the stream and that an entire group of sparrows splashed in shallow eddies, tending their feathers.

"Hey."

Malik's rich, masculine voice brought her turning away from the sink and the window.

She'd meant to greet him as well, but dammit if she didn't forget how handsome he was. And this time, with the apparent intention of supporting her journey through a domestic-bliss fantasy, the man helped her along by wearing jeans, a snug black t-shirt that accented his incredible body, and like her, he was barefoot.

She knew her lips were parted as she unabashedly checked him out. And she truly had meant to offer a greeting, but her mind couldn't seem to force the words from her throat.

His smile broadened. "You look beautiful."

"So do you," she gushed. "And you look great in jeans." That's when her cheeks heated up. She felt like a schoolgirl with a crush. "Uh, coffee?"

"Love some."

She poured him a large mug, which he took then sipped with his gaze fixed on her. And that's when his rich forest-like scent, like leaves in the fall burrowing into the earth to replenish the land, swept over her.

She turned the flame off beneath the bacon and pivoted in his direction.

When he set his coffee down, she opened her arms.

He moved so fast, she hardly saw him. But she felt him as he gathered her up in a powerful embrace and kissed her.

Willow slid her hands over his shoulders, his back, the muscles of his arms that flexed and un-flexed for her. She felt the raw physical power of him again, his strength covering her the way she covered the wraith colony.

When she parted her lips, he dipped his tongue inside and she leaned into him, cooing softly. The times they'd had sex slipped through her mind and she wanted him all over again, buried inside, driving into her, making her feel so many good things all at once.

But he drew back and took a deep breath. "You prepared breakfast and I'd hate to see it go to waste."

She looked into his eyes, searching their brown depths, wanting … what? "Right. Breakfast."

She released him and set about draining the bacon and serving up the frittata and sliced fruit.

The small dining area had a plate glass window overlooking the stream, and Malik's gaze went there often. Willow had a hard time not watching him as though she needed to memorize the angle of his cheekbones, how he turned his wrist when he lifted his mug to his lips, the set and breadth of his shoulders. She felt as though she was losing something infinitely precious, though she couldn't explain why she felt that way. He was right here, right in front of her.

But he couldn't be permanent. There just didn't seem to be a way to blend their worlds or their responsibilities into something that made sense.

After most of the meal had been consumed, she addressed an issue that had been on her mind since she'd awakened. "I want to bring the five leaders of the Fae Guild into the colony."

He shifted his gaze to her, his brows raised. "What? Why?"

She felt his sudden tension. "You think it would be a mistake?"

He gestured with his fork in the air. "I think the fewer the people who know about the colony, the safer we'll keep all those citizens. But tell me what you're thinking."

"That I need help and that you won't always be able to stick this close. You have the realm to think of. But as I told you last night, I've reached the absolute limit of my ability to serve as the Protector.

"I believe what I need is someone who can share the task with me. The five fae would probably be able to help out and they might also be able to locate another Protector. Maybe even one of them would have this ability."

Malik frowned as he settled his elbows on the table, his mug held in both hands. "I can't help but believe that we run a huge risk here. What if one of these fae is the woman that's supplying charms to Axton? I mean, I trust Alexandra the Bad with my life, but I don't know the other four as well at all."

"Then maybe I should lay the issue before her and let her make the call. Do I have your permission to contact her and tell her about the colony? Although, as I did with you, I'd prefer she actually experienced the colony for herself."

Malik leaned back in his chair, his gaze cast off to the side. She could feel how hard he was processing what she'd said, working through all the ramifications.

She thought she understood. He ruled Ashleaf and any decision made about the wraith colony would undoubtedly affect the realm for decades.

He glanced back at her. "Our being inside the colony changed things, didn't it?"

She nodded. "From the time I made the decision to include you, yes, I believe it did."

Malik rose from the table and picked up his dishes, taking them to the sink. Without a word, he started to clean-up, something that warmed her heart. Decades ago, she'd dated a few men who treated her like a scullery maid when it came to keeping the house tidy.

As she brought her dishes to the sink, he took them, saying, "Let me take care of those." And right then she knew she was in serious trouble with this man.

"Call Alexandra," he said, his gaze fixed out the kitchen window. "And do you know you have a colony of bats in that neighboring tree?"

"I do. I encourage them."

He cast his gaze down into the stream below. "You also have a battle going on in your stream involving about a dozen night-sparrows?"

She chuckled. "They love to bathe there and some insist on attempting to establish territorial rights."

At that, he smiled at her over his shoulder. "Sort of like I did with Axton."

She drew close and planted a kiss on his lips. "Yeah. Sort of like that. And now, I'm going to make my call."

She found her phone on the coffee table and sat down before dialing. She felt nervous calling Alexandra the Bad, who'd gained her reputation and the handle to her name several centuries ago. She'd routed a group of fae out of the Guild who'd been selling spells on the black market for all kinds of criminal and indecent activities.

Today, she'd be called a 'badass', so the nickname really fit.

"Alexandra? Willow here."

"Sweet merciful Goddess on high, how are you, my child?"

Willow laughed. "I'm eighty-three, hardly a child."

"No, I guess you're not. You've been on my mind lately, so tell me what's going on."

Willow laid it out for the older woman, including details about the colony that kept Alexandra very quiet. When she finally did make an utterance it was a very long expletive that involved a lot of terrible things she'd like to do to Axton.

When her tirade ended, she said, "Very well, tell me more about this colony."

When Willow finished, Alexandra muttered, "Why the fuck have I been kept in the dark? I don't think I've ever been so pissed in my life. I'm the head of the Fae Guild and sometime in the next century, I'll be sitting on the Sidhe Council. I'd be madder still if Malik hadn't also been treated like he was a worthless idiot."

"The decision was never mine," Willow explained. "The colony leadership had the final say and I always deferred to them."

Alexandra didn't speak for a moment, then, "Are you saying that you violated the leadership's directive by telling me these things?"

"I felt I had to bring Malik in and now you if we stand a chance of saving these wraiths. Axton is after them, but he's aligned with a fae of tremendous ability. I was hoping you could tell me if there's anyone in Ashleaf Realm with the kind of power to create charms that could burn up the Protector shield I've sustained all these decades. Maybe one of the black market fae?"

"I'm really not sure. As you know, we have a lot of fae who work in secret, so it's possible we're looking at one of them. But tell me, is the reason you haven't come to the meetings because you've been serving in this capacity all this time?"

"Of course it is. I've been sworn to secrecy. But in more recent years, I've found it increasingly difficult to hold the shield intact. I need your help, possibly even the assistance of the other four Fae Guild leaders."

"Sweet Goddess."

Alexandra fell silent again, and Willow let her be. She'd just unloaded a lot of information on the old fae's shoulders.

After a moment, Alexandra said, "One of my fae called this evening after having had a terrible vision about an explosion of white light in the very center of Ashleaf. Does that have any significance in this situation that you know of?"

Willow closed her eyes as her heart started to pound. "Only last night, Vojalie told Malik of a similar vision."

"Okay, that settles it. I'll bring the fae leadership with me. Just tell me when and where?"

Chapter Six

With the fae leadership scheduled to arrive in an hour, Malik flew Willow to the colony entrance where his Troll Brigade had held the ground throughout the daylight hours and where his Vampire Guard as well as Zane's force stood ready for orders.

With almost three hundred vampires on the ground, Malik immediately dismissed the Troll Brigade to retire for the night.

He watched, smiling, as the more jovial trolls high-fived the stern Vampire Guardsmen, which caused more than one friendly exchange that involved a proper amount of 'fuck you's'.

Zane stood at least twenty feet away in front of his Guard of fifty. He was slightly taller than Malik, muscled and lean and had a dagger tattoo on the right side of his neck, the image dripping with several red drops of blood. He wore his long black hair combed straight back in his Guardsman clasp and a diamond stud winked from his left earlobe. His cold light blue eyes surveyed his surroundings constantly. His nose was slightly aquiline, giving him a hawkish appearance, which suited his temperament.

He fought hard and played hard, and had a working stable of two dozen *doneuses* that he also took to bed on a regular basis.

Zane was a complete hard-ass and had more Invictus incursions in his land than any of the Nine Realms. He took no prisoners and thought Malik should have routed The Society with flamethrowers a long time ago.

He was as different from Malik as two men could be. But despite their opposing views, Malik considered Zane one of his closest friends; he trusted him with his life.

Zane lifted his hand in greeting, but sniffed the air, then shifted his penetrating gaze to Willow. He seemed to lean forward as though a wind pushed him from behind, then he simply fell to his knees. His mind beat against Malik's. *Get her away from me. Now.*

Willow gripped his arm. "You have to do something. I want to go to him. I can feel his blood-starvation like a burn on my skin."

The sight of the powerful Zane of Swanicott Realm in the dirt because Willow was a blood rose sent a shard of panic through Malik's skull.

"Malik!" Zane shouted. "You'd better figure this out, or I'm taking her. Now."

Malik turned to Willow, his mind whirling. All that came to him was her blood, that he needed it on him, though he had no idea why. "I have to bite you," he said quietly.

Willow's eyes fluttered, then fell to his lips. "Your fangs! Malik, sweet Goddess, do what you need to do."

Despite the audience, he took her wrist and bit swiftly. But instead of drinking he used his fingers and caught her blood, marking the backs of his hands and his throat in thin stripes. A vibration moved through him and through her and he could breathe again.

After he'd marked himself, he took a few sips, then sealed up the punctures with a swift lick of his tongue. He held Willow's gaze. "Better?"

"Much."

He turned toward Zane, hoping to hell this worked because he needed Willow beside him right now.

"Zane, will that do?"

Zane had his eyes closed, his hands on his thighs, breathing hard. He nodded several times. "Just give me a minute. Holy motherfucker that was raw."

Willow squeezed Malik's arm. *What made you think of marking yourself with my blood?*

I don't know. It just felt right, though I've never heard of it being done before. None of the conversations I've had with bonded mastyrs talked about this.

Well, whatever the reason, it worked. I can look at Mastyr Zane without feeling that overwhelming compulsion.

Thank the Goddess for that.

Malik glanced at all the Guardsmen and their general confusion. Many had turned away knowing they'd witnessed something way too private, while others looked horrified at what they'd just seen. He doubted many Guardsmen ever saw the effects of the blood rose phenomenon.

Zane rose to his feet and moved in Malik's direction to stand on his left. He looked shaken, and Malik knew exactly what that felt like. But it was also clear that the marking he'd done with Willow's blood, though temporary, would serve.

He turned to face both brigades, which were spread out in a wide arc and deep into the woods. He spoke in a loud voice. "We're facing an enemy we might not be able to see tonight. Mastyr Axton, who once ruled this realm, has been buying illegal fae charms in an attempt to break through this entrance that Mistress Willow has kept hidden." He gestured to the granite monolith behind him.

"On the other side of these vines live several wraith families that Willow has protected for decades. They are good realm-folk who tend to their homes and farms like the rest of Ashleaf's fine citizens. They deserve to be left in peace but for reasons that I think we all know, Axton has made it his mission to try to break through. And we have every reason to believe he will continue his efforts tonight.

"As most of you know, Axton also has a private Guard that I believe ranges close to one-hundred vampires strong and it's possible that this time, he'll bring them with him.

"We're here, above all else to offer protection to these innocent wraith families who deserve to be left alone. Will you serve Ashleaf in this way?"

A loud shout of accord went up.

He nodded, and when the cheer died down, he gave out his orders. Half the regiment took to the air and would patrol in a long line parallel to the vine covered entrance, spreading out over a couple of miles.

The rest moved into the forest a quarter mile deep. At the first sign of Axton or his men, three shouts in a row would alert the entire force.

The Guard was as prepared as it could be given the unknown circumstances of whatever spell Axton would bring with him this time.

To Zane, he said quietly, "Willow will take us through now."

Zane nodded, but didn't make eye-contact with Willow. The markings on Malik's hands had served to create just enough of a barrier, but Malik had a strong feeling it would still take so little to ignite the blood-rose craving between the two.

His own desire to smash Zane into a pulp kept roaring to life as well, but he drove it down. Zane needed to be here and the fate of the wraith colony might just depend on Zane having a good look at this part of the Nine Realms. Malik had once been to the wraith colony on Swanicott Island, but what existed here, in Ashleaf, was very different in nature and scope.

As before, Willow took them halfway through the tunnel, closed the vines behind, then opened the path before them.

"Shit, what is that light!" Zane cried out.

"It's not like the sun." Malik turned toward him. "It comes from the colony itself coupled with a connection to the earth."

"I don't get this at all."

"That's why I needed you here to see this."

When Zane saw the town square and all the normal activity, he shook his head repeatedly, hands on hips. "So this isn't just a few wraith families."

"A complete community of twenty thousand."

"Holy fuck. So many." A long curse followed.

Still holding Willow's hand, Malik let Zane have a good look and more importantly he gave him enough time to feel the vibrations that came from the Nine Realms.

When Zane finally looked down at his feet, his eyes were wide. "And what the hell is that?"

"We've been told by the Elders here in the colony that we're standing on the heartbeat of the Nine Realms where everything began." He didn't hold back either, but told Zane about the genome. "We're all part wraith."

Zane drew his lips back in a sneer. He wasn't a fan of wraiths because of the nature of the Invictus. During a battle, he never spared any of them. Even though Samantha, bonded to Mastyr Ethan of Bergisson Realm, had the power to dissolve the bonds that forged each wraith-pair, Zane had never once made use of her skills.

"This is fucking bullshit."

Malik didn't try to argue with him. Instead, he asked, "Is there room on Swanicott Island for them?"

"It would be cramped, but I don't think I care. Until the Invictus are gone from our world, wraiths ought to be policed to keep Margetta from adding to her army. And having them in one place would make our job easier, that's for sure."

"Zane, they're people."

"Who become killers if Margetta gets hold of them."

Malik knew he wouldn't change Zane's opinions, not with the Invictus still attacking innocent folk in every realm.

Zane turned to leave, then pivoted back and punched a finger in Malik's chest. "Do you want to know what I think?"

"Sure."

"I think the Ancient Fae is the one making these charms that keep disrupting Willow's shield, and I think Axton is in league with her. I'll bet you my last lay that they've been allies for the past two centuries. And somehow she found out about your wraiths and she wants them for her army."

"But Axton hates wraiths with a passion."

"That's true. But he wants Ashleaf back even more, which means he'd use Margetta if he thought it would help."

Malik had the worst feeling that Zane had called it right. All this time, he'd been thinking the source was one of the more powerful fae in his realm looking to make a buck by selling illegal charms. But it made a lot of sense that Margetta would be backing Axton. "If you're right, then we're in for it."

Zane glanced around once more, and swore under his breath as two wraith children, chasing each other, swooped in front of Zane, then darted away. "Damn, brats. Get me out of here before I do something I'll regret."

Willow led the way once more, and when Malik stepped out of the short tunnel, he saw that not only had the five fae women arrived, but a few of his Guardsmen were chatting up a couple of the younger ones who happened to be unattached.

Some things never changed.

Alexandra called to them sharply until all five were grouped around Malik. Willow greeted each of them with a kiss on the cheek.

If each woman glanced at the stripes of blood on Malik's hands and throat, no one said a word.

He called out to Evan and asked for a report. His response that all was quiet didn't surprise Malik. He felt certain that if Axton and one of his charms had gotten within even a mile of the colony, Willow would already have known.

Willow then led the leaders of the Guild back through the tunnel.

Alexandra the Bad walked closest to her. "The shield you've created is quite astonishing. I had no idea this was the path your powers had taken."

"I was well-instructed. The previous Protector trained me for five years before finally relinquishing her post."

When they moved into the town square, Malik was surprised to find that both Illiandra and Gervassay had arrived to greet the women. They hadn't shown the same courtesy to Zane, but then perhaps they knew his profound dislike of wraiths generally and chose to avoid him, at least for now.

All five fae immediately dropped to their knees and bowed their heads.

Malik leaned close to Willow. "What's going on?"

Willow turned to meet his gaze, but chose to path. *Remember that these women are the most powerful fae in your realm. They're feeling the heartbeat even now. They also understand that in the same way that I have protected the colony, Illiandra and Gervassay have guarded this central part of Ashleaf.*

Illiandra and Gervassay approached each of the women and laid hands on their foreheads. More blessings, maybe. Afterward, the fae rose and spoke quietly with the Elder wraiths.

Alexandra broke away and drew close to Willow once more, shaking a finger at her. "All this time I thought ill of you because you refused to attend meetings and to serve in the Guild. Instead, you were performing this critical service. I beg your pardon, Willow, for harboring uncharitable thoughts about you."

"But you couldn't have known, and I couldn't tell you."

Alexandra's bushy brows drew together. "But you were right to call me, my dear." She turned to Malik. "And you! Try not to be stupid, I beg of you. For as long as you are with Willow, you must treat her with the deepest respect. You have no idea what she's done for all of us."

"I do respect Willow. Tremendously."

She looked from one to the other. "So it's the blood rose phenomenon here, is it?"

Malik nodded.

"It is," Willow said.

But it was to Malik that Alexandra spoke, slapping his chest. "You need to wake up. You lack true understanding of what's needed in this situation."

Malik bristled. "I'm here, and I will protect Willow with my life. What more can I possibly do than that?"

Alexandra shook her head and this time placed a gentle hand on his chest. "Protect her, here. Here is what is important." She made a disgusted sound at the back of her throat. "Goddess save me from stupid men."

Willow intervened and shifted the subject. "Mistress, we're expecting an attack at any time. We should get you back through that you might return to your homes."

Alexandra pressed her lips together and shook her head. "If you think I would leave you now, when you've told me that you've reached a crisis in your ability to support the shield, you are greatly mistaken." She gestured behind her to the other women. "We will all stay and do what's required. This is the least we can do for you and for your wraiths."

~ ~ ~

Willow had never felt so relieved in her entire life. She was used to going it alone, and she couldn't believe Alexandra would respond so quickly and with a clear intent to help her.

"Thank you."

Alexandra nodded.

Suddenly, she felt Axton's presence but knew that he and a number of his private Guard were hidden behind a fae spell. She grabbed Malik's arm. "He's here."

Malik straightened his shoulders, a furrow between his brows. "Axton?"

Willow nodded. "With his Guard. But I doubt Zane or any of the others will be able to see any of them."

"I'll contact Zane." She watched Malik draw his cell from his leathers and make his call. He spoke quietly and laid out the situation, adding, "Yes, Willow's sure he's there with his men, but they're hidden." After a moment, he added, "Stay alert. This is it. We'll do what we can from this end to break the spell that's hiding him." He ended the call and put his cell away.

Willow weaved on her feet. "Malik, this one is going to be bad. I can feel the spell. Axton is winding up. Dear, sweet Goddess."

Despite the fact the night sky above the colony was perfectly clear, thunder rolled over the town and kept rolling.

"Axton," she said in a strong voice so that no one misinterpreted.

In response, Illiandra issued the now-familiar warning. The light that suffused the colony dimmed in gradual stages, and the same soft whistling sounded down the high street. All the wraiths, as they'd done the night before, disappeared swiftly into their shops and homes.

Willow could smell the smoke now. And the same acrid smell that came from the tunnel also streamed down from the sky above.

She trembled as she focused on her Protector power, but she felt as though her spell now contained a thousand rifts that would soon shatter the entire shielding frequency.

"Malik, this is more powerful than anything I've imagined. I need help. I can't hold this together."

Another crack of thunder and each fissure deepened, threatening to tear the shield apart.

From a distance she heard Malik's voice call to her. "Turn toward me. Face me. Open your eyes and look at me!"

When had she closed her eyes?

She forced them open and found that Malik had taken both her shoulders in hand and was inches away from her face, but she hadn't been aware of it. "Look at me!"

She glanced at his arms, but this time the power from the earth didn't flow as though blocked. She recalled that the intruder had taken her brush and she knew what had happened; she could feel a spell working against her.

She trembled now and sweat flowed. "Malik, there's a spell on me so that you can't channel the power through me like you did last night. Axton is going to break through any moment now. I don't know what to do."

"Use your fae-sisters. They're here to help." He turned to the Guild leaders. "Alexandra, you and the other fae surround Willow and touch her, connect with her. Willow's right. A charm is in place, blocking my ability to help funnel the earth's power. And if we're to save the colony, you have to find a way to add your power to hers, to us."

Willow could feel a third assault ready to strike and she knew it would destroy the shield. But at the same moment, Alexandra and the fae leadership touched her.

An arc of power caused her back to arch. She'd never felt anything like it before. She opened up quickly and let it flow. And just as another horrifying blast rocked the skies above, the power that she shared with the five women and with the heart of the Nine Realms below her feet, surged through her.

Countering the fae spell, the shared power burst heavily skyward and sealed up the damaged fissures. She felt every single breach refill and form a new, more powerful shell above the original shield.

"Stay with me," she called out.

She felt the answering response in the vibrations where each hand touched her as well as the power from the earth.

"Zane just pathed," Malik said. "He told me that the moment the shield rebuilt, Axton and his men became visible. They're battling right now just beyond the monolith and well into the forest."

"Thank the Goddess," Alexandra whispered.

Willow continued to stream their joint power and now that the protective shield was solid once more, she turned her attention to the vine entrance.

Focusing on the destroyed vines, she began rebuilding them and never had they reformed so quickly.

After a moment, she breathed a sigh of relief. "Everything is as it should be. The colony is safe. You can release me now."

Alexandra and the four remaining fae removed their hands. Willow tested the shield and found that it held, stronger than ever.

Malik let go of Willow as well, and the earth's vibration faded, returning to its usual soft humming sound.

She was left standing alone, her energy streaming to the shield. She felt both renewed and drained. A very odd sensation, but she smiled.

Malik addressed all the women. "Zane reported in again. Axton fled with his force after losing two of his bodyguards and eight regular troops." He then smiled. "My Vampire Guard and Zane's suffered only minor injuries."

Willow smiled at this news as well and all five fae gave a shout of rejoicing.

"Thank you," she said, holding Malik's gaze. "Thank you." She then turned and said the same thing to Alexandra and each of the fae.

"Of course," Alexandra said, frowning.

"Is something wrong?" Willow asked.

"Not sure why you're thanking us? You're the one that saved the wraith colony just now."

"No, that's not true. I almost lost it. If I hadn't had all of you with me, as well as the frequency that came from the realm heartbeat, the shield would have been destroyed."

Alexandra shook her head and leaned in to place a kiss on Willow's cheek. Her gaze then slid to Malik. "You'd be a fool to let this one go. Mark my words, stupid man."

Illiandra and Gervassay approached them and celebrated by also offering a round of hugs and cheek-kissing. Illiandra then invited everyone to their villa for a celebratory dinner.

Willow agreed readily and was grateful that the fae leadership would be joining them. Though everyone seemed so certain that the new level of power that had been added to the protective shield wouldn't readily be pierced, Willow wasn't so sure.

Malik, however, needed to speak with Zane and the combined troops and asked if Willow would take him through to the entrance.

Malik would want to be with his men. "Of course."

She left him there with the understanding that she would return to fetch him when he was ready.

~ ~ ~

Malik listened to Zane's recounting of the battle, frustrated that again they had seen nothing of Axton and his men until the new charm's spell had been repulsed.

"He'd brought a hundred men," Zane said, his voice low. "But we never saw any of them or Axton who was busy trying to destroy the vines at the entrance. I'm still stunned that I couldn't see a damn thing."

Malik frowned. He was grateful they'd thwarted this attack, especially without losing any of his men or Zane's. But if Zane was right and Margetta was behind Axton, what else would she throw at them?

A clean-up crew had arrived to remove the corpses to a morgue. Malik didn't recognize any of the deceased, so they'd probably been with Axton for the last couple of centuries.

Zane shook his head. "Axton was thrown to the ground when the spell reversed, as though a wave of power hit him. I almost had him, but his bodyguards rushed in. Two of them died." He waved a hand in the direction of the stretchers.

Malik still felt an echo of the power that had traveled among the fae and from the earth. He glanced at the corpses, at the vines now healed at the entrance, at the combined force of his men and Zane's together.

This was where he belonged, in command of his men, in support of his fellow realm ruler, in charge of keeping Ashleaf safe. He didn't want to lose sight of that. The all-encompassing feelings of what existed between Willow and himself, of what the bond would require of him, gave him serious pause. How much would he risk if he completed the bond with Willow?

"How do you want to handle this?" Zane asked. "I think you need to arrest Axton. You have cause. Insurrection, for one thing."

Malik knew another hard truth about the situation. Because Axton had already shown his cards, he wouldn't be easy to find.

Switching to telepathy, he tapped Zane's frequency.

Zane pathed, *Telepathy. Probably a good idea.* He glanced around at the night sky and the surrounding forest. *Who the hell knows if we're being observed or listened to?*

Malik turned toward Zane, facing him fully. *I want you to send a black-ops team to try to find Axton. That way he won't be on the alert that we're on his heels. But yeah, I need to arrest him, no matter what the fall-out is in Ashleaf.*

You think whatever charm hid him here will also protect him in his home?

I do. You'll have to catch him, if possible, when he's not using a spell.

He's smart, that asshole, but I'll get on it. Zane gestured to the fall of vines. *So, what happened in the colony?*

Malik told him everything.

Shit. Your woman has so much power. What are you going to do? Are you going to bond with her?

Malik shrugged, but held Zane's gaze. *I don't know. Neither of us wants this.*

Zane frowned at him. *I've heard about the resistance to the bond over and over. Why is that?*

But Malik could only laugh and finally spoke aloud. "I think the biggest reality is that it's so damn permanent. To my knowledge, it can't be broken. Try that on for size when it hits you with whatever woman happens to have the gift. In this case, I haven't really spoken to Willow in decades and suddenly, she's a blood rose."

Zane kicked at the dirt, his arms tight over his chest. "Is it true about the blood-starvation? Gone, just like that?"

"It's true."

"Shit."

"Yep."

"Well, you'd better decide fast. Even I was drawn to her, which means Axton has to be thinking about her all the time."

Malik grimaced. "No doubt."

"Then stick close to her, because it would be a tragedy if he somehow got hold of her and forced a bond."

Malik nodded. But because the thought was so distressing, he found a compartment within his brain, shoved it in there, then locked the door tight.

He changed the subject. "We're having an informal celebration dinner inside the colony. Why don't you come?"

At that, a haunted look entered Zane's eye. "I know you mean well, but you know how I feel about wraiths."

"Yeah. I do." He wanted to encourage Zane to explore the colony, but Zane had been hard hit by the Invictus in his realm and didn't have a lot of sympathy for wraiths.

Zane glanced around. "Besides, I can take care of things here, with both brigades, while you're doing your thing inside the colony."

Malik had never felt more grateful. "Thanks, Zane. Your help tonight has been tremendous on every front."

Zane almost cracked a smile. He tugged at his diamond stud instead and told Malik to fuck off.

Malik laughed, then contacted Willow. Within a few minutes, she reappeared at the vine entrance. He went to her quickly and disappeared within, taking her hand as she waved the vines away repeatedly.

When he emerged in the town square, the light was back and many realm-folk once more stood on the street cheering them as before. Again, he was overwhelmed by such a strong outpouring of love and gratitude. He wished Zane was here to see this, to feel how different the people in the colony were from the Invictus wraith-pairs.

As he walked along, however, he became acutely aware of Willow. Zane had planted a seed about Axton trying to get his hands on Willow, and the roots had gone deep. He felt a profound need to stick close just as Zane had suggested.

He released her hand, offering his arm.

She seemed a little surprised, but when she took it, wrapping her arm around his, he caught her rain-in-the-forest scent and his desire for her rose swiftly. He also realized he needed to feed from her vein, and that his part in restoring the shield had drained him.

I can feel your hunger, she pathed, waving to a group of wraith children clustered at an upper story window.

I want to be with you again, Willow. Would that be acceptable to you?

She shifted and met his gaze, searching his eyes. *Very. You have to know I want you as well. My wraith fangs have been vibrating softly from the moment I returned to the vine entrance.* Her gaze fell to his throat where the protective lines of her blood still remained visible on his skin.

The thought of her small, sharp fangs burrowed anywhere on his body, shrunk his pants. At least the Guardsman coat could hide that sin, but he worked to calm himself. *I'll try to make our excuses early.*

Good plan, because I want to take you to my pool.

Sweet Goddess, her pool.

He barely repressed a groan as they finally arrived at the villa. He stopped her at the top of the path to the front door and turned her to face him. "You mean the pool where I often watched you bathe?"

She smiled softly and he could see that her cheeks wore a blush, again. "Yes, that pool. I liked you watching me, Malik. I always knew when you were there."

"You did? Then you were tormenting me on purpose?"

"But you did the same to me. I've been hungry for you for so long, and now that we've been working together, I want you all the more. It's as though I can feel you vibrating inside me here." She touched her chest, which of course drew his gaze to the line of her cleavage.

Knowing that the last of the townsfolk to cheer them on were now at least a hundred yards away, he took her in his arms and kissed her.

She cooed softly, parting her lips and allowing him entrance.

He drove his tongue gently, but in steady thrusts so that she knew exactly what he wanted to be doing to her right now.

After a moment, he drew back. "I wish I could take you away right now."

"Me, too."

He glanced at the house, all lit up inside with a couple dozen candles. "I suppose it would be rude."

She chuckled. "That, and they'd all know what we meant to do. I'm sorry, Malik, but that would be too embarrassing."

He laughed with her as he turned her to walk down the path. But he had to take it slow so that his cock could ease back.

Caris Roane

When he finally crossed the threshold, they were each pulled away in different directions, being introduced to more of the colony's leadership. But Malik always knew where she was. Now that they'd agreed on what would happen next, his body had zeroed in on her.

He caught her eye often, and when they sat beside one another at dinner, he kept his hand on her knee and more than once she told him telepathically how arousing it was for her to have his hand there.

Finally, the time came when they could politely leave, the Fae Guild members with them.

Willow guided them all out through the vines and bid the Fae goodnight. Alexandra once more yelled at him about needing to bond with Willow. He responded by kissing the woman on the cheek. The truth was, he didn't know what to do; it all felt way too soon for that kind of commitment.

She grunted. "Be smart, warrior."

When all five fae disappeared into the woods, Malik gathered Willow up in his arms and flew her in the direction of her sacred pool.

Arriving at the waterfall, he touched down on the granite slab at the opposite end and set her on her feet. "I can feel your power all around here. And something more, something that I've felt in the wraith colony."

She glanced down at her feet. "I know what you mean. I think the heart of the Nine Realms lives here as well." She turned in a circle, waving her arms to encompass the surrounding dense forest, the moss at the base of the north-facing trees, the ferns, the fifteen foot waterfall that spanned at least ten feet off a sheer drop

170

of granite. "This was my secret place until you showed up. I often feel as though I'm reborn here."

"I get that. I really do."

He slipped out of his Guard coat and shirt then found a flat rock to sit on to start working off his snug, thigh boots.

She watched him for a moment, then moved to kneel in front of him on the surrounding grass. She took his boot at the heel and eased the leather off his foot. She helped with the second boot and all he could think was that this one act defined Willow; she was always willing to help.

Standing up, he stripped out of his leathers, revealing his half-aroused state. The entire world seemed to grow quiet as he stood before her completely naked.

She slid her hands over his pecs, then moved slowly around his waist to cup his buttocks. He was breathing hard when she drifted her hands forward to his lower abdomen and took him gently in hand, stroking him. "You have a beautiful cock, Malik."

His chest swelled at the compliment. "All for you."

She nodded and stepped away from him, tugging her tank off. The sight of her breasts mounded because of her bra almost set his feet in motion, his fingers itching to touch her. But he held back, because he sensed she wanted him just to watch right now. Reaching behind, she unhooked her bra and freed her breasts.

His mouth watered and his tongue rimmed his lips. After all that had happened, he needed this, needed to be with her, to take a breath and sink into the simple pleasure of sex.

She slipped off her shoes and socks then slowly peeled her jeans and her thong down her body. By the time she'd set her clothes aside, Malik could hardly breathe. Whatever a man's naked body did for a woman, he couldn't imagine it was more than what he felt right now.

Willow had a beautiful figure, her hips swelling in just the right way, her ass firm, her breasts large and round. He longed to bury his face between them. Yet still he waited, wanting Willow to have her pleasure, to have this moment unfold in a way that would please her.

This was her land, a place that strengthened her.

And he was right, because when she approached him, she took his hand. "Come swim with me. I want you to feel what this water is like. I think it will surprise you."

She drew him to the end of the granite slab. He felt oddly lightheaded as she directed him to stand with his back to the water just on the edge of the stone.

"Don't worry, Malik, the water is very deep here. Just fall with me."

Just *fall* with her. Did that have another meaning as well?

He had hold of her hand as he stared up into the starry night sky. A breeze whipped the tree-canopy around so that a feeling of the wild ran through him. His blood stirred.

Standing beside him, also facing away from the water, she took hold of his hand. "Just fall on three. One … two … three …"

He let himself go, a feeling so unfamiliar that when he hit the water, he felt just as she said that in some strange way he was being reborn. The heart of the Nine Realms had him right now, holding him as he fell into the dark depths of the pool, sinking deeper and deeper.

She still held his hand and gave another squeeze. He understood her intention and pushed toward the surface just as she did.

When he broke through, he took a deep breath and drank in the night air. "This feels incredible as though something magical lives in these waters."

"I know." She paddled slowly away from him.

As he treaded water, the vibrations in the pool began to work on his mating frequency deep in his chest. He slowly began to move through the water in Willow's direction, driven as he had been for the past two years because she was a blood rose and he needed what she had to give.

Yet the drive had expanded, filling his mind as well, even his soul because this was Willow, a woman he'd come to respect for the sacrifices she had made and for her courage.

She pulled herself with an elegant backstroke in the direction of the waterfall.

He glanced up, his lips beneath the waterline. Had the vines always been there? Maybe, but several now trailed in the water in her direction.

More vines … yes.

His cock hardened at the thought.

Maybe it was the pool, or his connection to Willow, but he suddenly realized what he could do. He reached for the vines mentally and they responded to him. He knew exactly what he wanted to have happen and maneuvered them in Willow's direction until they wrapped around her arms and held her fast.

She gasped as she rose up in the water, the vines holding her up as she faced him.

"The vines are doing my bidding," he explained.

She smiled. "I can see that."

More of them caught her arms and supported her until she was partway out of the water, but half-reclining, her head cradled on a small bed of vines. The sight of her bare breasts, her nipples peaked in the cool air, prompted another idea.

He thought the thought and more vines appeared, diving deeper this time until they wrapped around her thighs and spread them.

He moved closer and ran his hands below the waterline, up the insides of her legs. He loved having the vines work for him, following his thoughts, his desires, until her hips were also above the waterline. Vines now covered her abdomen, keeping her warm, and supporting her.

Slowly, he kissed his way up her thighs, taking turns with each, holding her hips and kneading her bottom. As he reached the juncture of her thighs, he kissed the narrow auburn landing patch, then flipped his tongue back and forth.

"Oh, Malik." She tilted her head back and he went to work, licking her between her legs and making her writhe in the water.

He stood on bedrock, positioned well to taste her sweet forest-rain scent and suck on her labia.

She moaned, her hips rising and falling in the ancient rhythm. He slid a finger inside her beautiful wetness and added a vibration that had her crying out. "Oh, sweet Goddess."

He could feel that she was close. He licked her swiftly and plunged his finger in and out. Her body tensed then a long cry left her lips as ecstasy caught her and took her on a ride. He could feel her internal muscles fluttering as she came.

He was hard as a rock because of the sensation, then he felt a vine rubbing over his thighs and ass. *You're doing that, aren't you?* He pathed.

The vine, yes. How does it feel?

He moved in close to her, spreading his hands up over her breasts. "It feels wonderful because it has your frequency."

She nodded, still trapped and held up by the vines. "Move into me, Malik. Let me feel you, all of you."

He stepped between her thighs and holding his cock in his hand, he began pushing into her, and started thrusting while she uttered small cries of pleasure. The vines gave way a little as she shifted her legs to surround him.

When he commanded more support, the vines formed a stronger platform beneath her and he set a steady rhythm. "How does that feel?"

She moaned. "Wonderful." She held his gaze, her hips meeting his with each thrust. "Malik, I love doing this with you, feeling you inside me." Her neck arched and she writhed once more.

He added a soft vibration to his cock.

She gasped. "Oh, Sweet Goddess, that's amazing." She panted now, her mouth open. He leaned over and kissed her, dipping his tongue inside. She responded, her own tongue flicking against his, making him harder still.

He sped up his thrusts and watched her roll her head as she gasped for breath.

Finally, she caught the back of his neck. "Wait."

He slowed the rocking of his hips. "Tell me what you want. Anything, Willow. Anything."

She smiled faintly, her lips swollen, passion on every feature. "There's something I want to do to you. I've fantasized about it. Will you allow it?"

The thought of fulfilling one of her fantasies made his cock twitch. "I'll do whatever you want."

"Then take me back over to the granite slab."

When her fangs showed, he groaned. He withdrew from her and at the same time all the vines drifted away.

She swam ahead of him. "Come with me." She had the slightest, sexiest lisp because of her wraith-fangs, and his whole body vibrated with the need for her to use them. Anywhere.

She patted the granite. "Climb up here and get comfortable, but dangle your legs in the water."

He felt the vines moving around him, only this time, she commanded them. As he stretched himself out and spread his legs for her, he thought maybe somewhere in this pool he'd died and gone to heaven.

~ ~ ~

Willow ordered the vines to build a support beneath her feet since the water was very deep where it met the granite. With a platform of vines holding her up, she came up part way out of the water and ran her hands up Malik's oh-so-muscular thighs.

Maybe being with a warrior hadn't been what she'd imagined for herself, but the physical reality proved superb.

Her fingers trembled as she felt the latent physical strength in his legs. She drew close and licked his firm cock all the way up to the crown. She took the head in her mouth and with her hands, just felt him up: his thighs, his buttocks, anywhere she could reach.

He groaned heavily, her cue to move things along.

She shifted slightly to his right pelvis area and began licking the skin above his vein. She knew exactly where she wanted to drink from him. With one hand curled around his cock and fondling him gently, she felt his vein rise. She kept licking the area, adding short little jabs of her tongue, until the vein was right there ready for her. She angled her head and with a quick strike bit down.

His whole body jerked as he cried out. She settled in and began to suck.

His blood. His blood. His blood.

The sweet elixir tasted of the rich forest, and of the earth where all good things grew.

She moved her hand up and down his stalk, his hips arching in response.

His blood powered her body, and she wanted more.

So much more.

While she drank, she shifted her gaze to him and saw that he'd lifted up on his elbows. His lids were low as he watched her drink, his gaze moving from her lips as she suckled, to her hand that still stroked his erect cock.

Malik, do you like what I'm doing?

He nodded slowly, his lips parted. "I could come so easily like this." His deep voice filled the whole space, sending a thrill through her abdomen.

She continued for a full minute, watching his nostrils begin to work like bellows as his breathing grew harsh.

But she'd become needful again and left his vein, licking the small holes, sealing them up. She had the vines lift her out of the water so that he could see her head to toe. "Take me, Malik, however you want me. Just take me."

Her words had a powerful effect, because the water around her rose in a great swell. The vines she'd been using vanished and she was suddenly caught up in his arms. He levitated and swept her onto her back on the granite, but she landed on a soft cushion of vines.

She wrapped her arms around his neck and held on tight as he found his way inside her again, pushing in erotic thrusts that caused her back to arch and a new set of cries to leave her throat.

Sex had never felt like this, as though with his cock buried deep, she was taking in every part of life. She truly felt one with the forest around her, with the land she loved, and with her sacred pool.

The vines caressed her as Malik embraced and fondled her, mirroring the way he made love to her, creating sensation on sensation.

Her body poised and ready, she panted now as ecstasy rose once more.

At the same time, she felt his hunger and she rolled her neck, presenting her throat. He gave a small, hungry shout, then licked a line up her neck. Because her vein throbbed, he pierced her quickly and began to suck.

The two sensations, his cock moving rapidly in and out and his mouth suckling at her neck, had her trembling with the need for another release. *Malik, I'm ready.*

I can feel that you are, but wait, just for a minute. I want to come with you.

With short quick breaths, she held the orgasm at bay, but she so ready. He sent a soft vibration through his cock and another at her neck.

"Oh, Malik." She whimpered between pants.

Almost there. The thrusts grew deeper, his cock harder.

Suddenly, he released her neck, his eyes boring into hers. "Come with me, Willow."

"Malik, sweet Goddess."

He nodded and she fell straight over the edge as pleasure streaked through her, rising and swelling, pushing through her chest, until her mind filled with stars once more.

And just as the wave crested, Malik moved vampire fast and another orgasm followed, stronger this time. Her cries echoed around the forest, until she was trembling and the sensations began to ease back.

"You're beautiful when you come, Willow. Now let's do it once more."

She didn't know if she could handle so much pleasure, but Malik sped up his thrusts and a third incredible wave rolled through her, spinning her around and around, until she was crying out over and over.

Malik released at the same time, shouting into the night air, sending more thrilling shards of ecstasy scorching her deep within and bringing her cries pounding against Malik's own roars thundering into the night.

The vines whipped around them both in wild tandem with their shared pleasure and the water rose as well in waves that washed over them repeatedly.

When the last of the orgasm faded, she had her arms flung on the granite above her head, her chest rising and falling. Malik lay on top of her, still connected, breathing hard.

Her eyes were closed and the vines began to slip away, disappearing into the water and retreating to hang once more on either side of the waterfall.

She'd gone into the wilderness and returned. She felt moved, deeply so. And changed.

She wanted to say something, to give some sort of verbal expression to all that she felt, but she couldn't.

Instead, she surrounded Malik's heavily-muscled shoulders with her arms and held him tight.

The words came at last. "That was so beautiful, Malik. I never thought it could be like this. Ever. I felt one with the pool, the vines, the granite, the earth, our world."

"You've said it just right. And did you feel the waves?"

"Yes, the water rose up and kept washing over us."

He sighed. "It was the most magnificent sensation. I was releasing and you were crying out. This was beyond anything I could have imagined."

"Malik, together we seemed to be so connected to everything around us."

"It's you. I know it's you."

She hugged him. "Actually, I think it's how we are together. I know I have a vine-gift, but I've never moved the water."

As Malik remained resting inside her, a new emotion moved through her chest, warming her, swelling her heart and bringing tears to her eyes. Was it possible that during all this time, beginning with so many chases through the forest, she'd been falling in love with him?

Or maybe it went back farther, back to appreciating all that Malik was as the ruler of Ashleaf Realm, the man who instituted laws that saved lives, the man that fought prejudice wherever he found it, the same man who helped her to engage with the five fae so that together they succeeded in healing the protective shield over the colony.

Whatever the case, how she felt about Malik had layers and texture, like the vines that had held them together, like the water that had seemed to come alive and flow over them while they made love.

Maybe she didn't understand all that was happening to her, but one question rose: after all that had happened, how could she ever let him go?

Chapter Seven

Later, Malik flew Willow back to her house. After showering and cleaning up, he helped her make pastrami sandwiches, then suggested they grab a couple of beers and take their meal to the meditation porch. She agreed with a smile. That she wanted to kick back was exactly what he needed, and the thought crossed his mind that Willow was so his kind of woman.

Settling into his chair, he contacted Evan first to make sure that all was in order at the entrance to the colony. Evan confirmed that he had half the Ashleaf Vampire Guard as well as all of Zane's force on duty patrolling in the air and on the ground. They couldn't control whether Axton returned while cloaked behind yet another invisibility charm, but he had his vampires in place no matter what Axton threw at them.

Malik felt in his bones that Axton wouldn't make another attempt tonight, but he wanted all the bases covered. Willow held the same sentiment, so he delivered a few standard orders about keeping on the alert and of course for rotating the Troll Brigade at dawn. After he hung up with Evan, he called Zane, talking everything over with him as well.

Zane held a similar opinion about Axton, but said he'd be staying in Ashleaf for a couple of nights just in case. "Are you with Willow?"

Malik glanced at her. "I am. Through the night."

Zane chuckled low then told him to stay right where he was and that he and Evan would look after both Vampire Guards.

Malik rarely set his duties aside to be with a woman. But Willow was a helluva lot more than just sex and more maybe than he wanted to admit, so he didn't fight Zane too hard.

With his mind at ease, Malik took Willow to bed and made love to her again. The vines crept over the windowsill once more and bound them together, creating a wild paradise on her soft cotton sheets. This time, he slowed things down and worked every part of her body, taking from more than one vein and giving her the opportunity to pierce him as many times as she wanted as well.

Maybe because she, too, felt that their time together would be limited, she took advantage of his suggestion and bit him in at least five different places until he shook with need. He had to admit he'd never spent such an erotic night with a woman in his life. He supposed they'd both been so bereft of meaningful relationships that something hungry had been released.

Near dawn, Malik held her in his arms, but felt her disquiet.

"Something's bothering me," she murmured.

"You mean about us? About being together?"

Smiling, she lifted up off his chest just enough to meet his gaze. "No, not at all. I've never been so content. I just feel as though I missed something, or I didn't read Axton or the charm right. Something."

He patted her shoulder. "I have no doubt you always feel this way."

At that, she sighed deeply and collapsed on his chest. "You're right. I'm worried most of the time."

"Well, you don't have to be right now. I'm here."

At dawn, he fell asleep with his arms still holding her close and wishing he could stay there forever.

When he woke up hours later, however, Willow was no longer in bed and panic hit him hard. *Willow?*

I'm fine. I'm making oatmeal. What's with the stress?

He took a deep breath. Sweet Goddess, he was on edge. *You weren't in bed with me. I got worried.*

He felt her silence and thought something was off about that. *Are you sure you're all right?*

Just a headache, but I'm working on it.

A headache? He thought this odd since most powerful fae had tremendous self-healing abilities. Of course, they'd both been under the gun.

Breakfast will be ready in a few minutes. It's almost full-dark.

Thanks. I'll be there after I shower.

He shut down the communication and stared up at the finely crafted wood ceiling of Willow's bedroom treehouse, Hank's original work. He still couldn't believe he was here, in Willow's home, having made love to her repeatedly.

Whatever the night had been, however, his mind reverted to his duties as Mastyr of Ashleaf, especially the need to make sure that not one more half-breed fell victim to The Society. And with Zane here, he could begin the process of moving at-risk families to Swanicott Island.

With full-dark almost on him, his need to get back to his Vampire Guard built within him like a mounting pressure inside his chest. He shaved and showered, then brushed his long hair out, pulling it back in the woven Guardsman clasp. He hoped to hell that Zane's black ops force had been able to track Axton down. Malik no longer cared what kind of repercussions resulted from arresting Axton. With a growing concern that he might be in league with the Ancient Fae, Malik had no other choice.

And right now, he longed to be heading out in pursuit of Axton, rather than waiting here with Willow.

By the time he sat down to breakfast with her, he'd made up his mind to get back to his Vampire Guard.

"Malik, what's going on? I can feel that you're about ready to jump out of your skin."

He met her gaze. "I'm sorry, Willow, but I have to get back to work."

She leaned forward slightly. "Of course, and I have no problem with that. It might even help."

At that, he poured milk on his oatmeal. "Why's that?" He frowned at her. She had dark circles beneath her eyes. "Are you okay?"

She rubbed her forehead. "I've got a headache this evening, and I'm having trouble focusing."

"Didn't you sleep last night?"

"Not much. I kept waking up with that same sense of having left something undone, but for the life of me I can't figure out what it was." She added a few raisins and brown sugar to her cereal.

He'd never been that tight with any of the fae, so maybe headaches on occasion came with the job description. Although, with all that she'd been through, no wonder she hadn't slept very well.

But he also thought he needed to address at least one critical issue and to finally come clean about her father's death. "Listen, there's something I need to talk over with you, Willow. I hope that's okay."

She looked up at him, wincing slightly and rubbing her temple once more. "Yes, please. Tell me anything you want. I mean that."

For a moment, however, he couldn't speak, couldn't quite bring himself to say what needed to be said, because he really liked Willow. In fact, he liked everything about her.

But he squared his shoulders anyway. "First, I'm not inclined to complete the bond with you. At least not now. I have too damn much on my plate."

She let out a heavy huff of air. "I am so with you. I mean, I've loved having you in my bed and what we experienced in the pool together was amazing. But the Ashleaf Colony has to come first. I owe that to the memory of my parents and to every life born under my watch."

They shared the same level of obligation so that once again he hesitated. Part of him felt an overwhelming need to stick close. But the other part demanded he get back to his men and to the larger concerns of his realm. "If our circumstances had been different," he offered.

She rested her chin in the palm of her hand. "I know. I'd totally go out with you if I was just a regular fae."

"And I'd ask you out if I weren't Mastyr of Ashleaf." But his conscience once more prompted him to make a clean breast of things. "But I'm not sure you'd say yes if you knew everything."

At that, she lifted her head and eased back against her chair, dropping her hands into her lap. "What do you mean?"

Now his head started to hurt. "There's something else that must be said. Something I have to tell you about the night your father died."

She grew very still. Her hazel eyes widened.

"Shit, I don't even know how to say this. I've hated that this moment would come, but maybe it's for the best."

"Malik, I have the worst feeling—"

"As you should." He took the horrible plunge. "I was the one who killed your father that night."

Her fingers went to her lips. "Oh, Malik, no. Not you. Anyone but you." Tears filled her eyes.

"I should have told you sooner, but how could I? Few situations have hurt me as much as taking the life of a good, honest, hard-working man like your father." He rushed on, "But he was deranged with grief. My squad had cornered him because he was threatening the lives of a troll family thought to be part of The Society. They weren't, of course, but he wanted revenge. I tried to talk him down, but he held a knife to the troll's throat. I only used my battle frequency at the very last moment, a killing shot to the head. As it was, the troll almost died."

There, he'd said the ugly truth about what had happened.

Willow covered her face with her hands, resting her elbows on the table once more. He saw tears slide down her chin from beneath her fingers. "I always knew the killing had been justified, but it really hurts that it was you."

For a long moment, Malik stared at her, knowing he should do something to try to comfort her. But what rolled through his mind was that the time had come to step back from the whole blood rose situation.

He stood up and pushed his chair in, his chest aching for reasons he didn't fully understand. He wanted to keep apologizing but what good would that do?

"If I could undo this, if there'd been any other way … " He remembered seeing the blood spurt from the troll's neck; he'd reacted instinctively when he'd killed her father.

Dropping her hands, she lifted her face to him, eyes watery. "I believe you. I do." More tears, then once more she rubbed her forehead.

He sighed deeply. "I'm going to send two squads to serve as your private security detail."

She just nodded. "I'm sure that would be best."

The thought of Axton getting anywhere near her, though, had him shuddering.

He'd keep the detail on her until he and Zane had run Axton to ground. In an emergency, Willow could send for Malik and he'd do whatever was needed to continue protecting the wraith colony or to prevent Axton from getting his hands on her. Even if Axton approached her because he bore an invisible spell, Willow could still alert the guards.

Right now, however, he needed to get back to business.

He contacted Evan and made the arrangements.

Afterward, he carried his bowl to the sink and slowly cleaned it. He'd only taken a couple of bites. "Thank you for the oatmeal." A strange kind of dullness filled his chest.

"Don't worry about the dishes." Her voice sounded empty.

He returned to the table, and glancing out the front window, he saw the squads had landed on the path in front of her house. "My men are here, and I have to go."

But she wouldn't look at him.

Guilt pummeled him once more. "Willow, I'm so sorry. I've had to live with this all these decades. If I'd had any other recourse –"

At that, she met his gaze and at the same time rose to her feet. "I ... I was never comfortable with your warrior lifestyle, Malik, so maybe it's best to have things end right now. This was never a viable arrangement."

"Willow." No words followed because he didn't know what to say; he'd made his decision. Oddly, his chest started hurting in the worst way.

Part of him wanted to pull her into his arms, but once more he felt an incredible pressure to get back to his Guardsmen. "I'll send someone to gather up my things."

She nodded, wiping another stray tear from her cheek.

He left by way of the front door, and after issuing orders to the Guardsmen, he flew swiftly up above the canopy of the dense forest, then sped back to his house.

He contacted Zane mind-to-mind, asking about the black ops team, but they'd had no luck through the previous night locating Axton. Malik was disappointed, but not especially surprised.

A few minutes later, he landed on the front walk of his home, then opened the door. But the moment he crossed the threshold, a strange dizziness passed through his head that made him pause. Once the sensation drifted away, he tried to take a step forward, but couldn't. In fact he couldn't move at all. What the fuck?

He tried to call out to his housekeeper, but even his voice was frozen.

Mentally, he reached out for Zane, but he couldn't path, not to Zane, not to anyone.

Panic set in so that for the next couple of minutes he did everything he could think of to either move his feet or to reach someone telepathically but nothing worked.

It didn't take a genius to figure out what had happened. Right now he was caught in a powerful fae spell. To his knowledge, not even Alexandra the Bad could create a stasis spell, which meant that Zane's was right after all.

And Margetta had come for him.

He thought about Willow's headache, her uneasiness, and that she hadn't slept well. Dammit, if he hadn't been so caught up in leaving her, he might have figured out that something *fae* had been at work in her treehouse as well, disturbing her dreams and causing her pain.

Another wave of panic flowed through him. He didn't have to be told that right now Axton was already inside Willow's home and that Malik couldn't do a damn thing about it because he was trapped in his own house.

~ ~ ~

Willow hadn't moved from the time that Malik left. Instead, she sat with her elbows on the table, her head in her hands. She'd never experienced such a bad headache in her life and no amount of self-healing seemed to offer any relief. It was as though someone was pounding on her telepathic frequency demanding admittance, yet when she searched the vibration, nothing was there.

But there was something more. She regretted letting Malik leave without assuring him that she didn't blame him for killing her father. She had just been so taken aback by his confession, that she hadn't been able to process it quickly enough. And Malik had looked so stricken when he'd told her, but he'd left before she could tell him that she really did understand and that he was forgiven. She'd had decades to come to terms with what had happened.

She rubbed her temples, wishing the headache would let up.

Then suddenly, the pain was gone. But why?

"Hello, Willow. Sweet Goddess but you smell like heaven."

Willow looked up. "Oh, no."

Axton.

She glanced around. He appeared to be alone, yet she could feel a powerful fae presence supporting him. And just like that, she understood the whole picture, why she hadn't slept well and why she'd had a headache and why the pain had just now vanished; she'd been under a terrible spell and now the spell had been broken.

In its stead, however, a great evil had entered her treehouse.

Margetta the Ancient Fae, the creator of the Invictus scourge, had come to call.

"Take her," a female voice whispered along the air currents of the room.

She rose to her feet, wanting to face the enemy while standing. "You've been behind all of this, Mistress Margetta?" She glanced around the space, looking for any sign of the woman.

"Of course." The voice had a wavy, disguised sound, as though cloaked, a protective spell, maybe, that kept her hidden. "And all I needed to do was to wait for Malik to leave you as I knew he would.

"I want the wraiths in that little colony you've been hiding and I mean to have each and every one. They'll make a fine army and Axton intends to help me pair them up with the willing citizens of The Society. Now isn't that a match made in heaven?"

Willow's heart raced. There had to be a way out of this mess, but how? And already her desire for Axton began to swell within her. The blood rose gift was anxious to feed any mastyr vampire who drew near.

Then a golden light appeared, and Margetta made herself visible. Willow turned toward her and gasped. The woman was so beautiful for someone with such a twisted soul. She had long blond hair, a lovely straight nose and wide-set, violet eyes.

"You're Margetta the Ancient Fae."

"I am."

She waved a hand toward Willow that froze her in place. She'd heard rumors that the most powerful fae could create a stasis spell, but she'd never felt one before.

Margetta drew close to Axton and took his hand, leading him toward Willow.

Willow tried to back up, to move away, to run, but she was paralyzed. She tried to scream, but her voice was frozen as well.

When the Ancient Fae took Willow's hand, a powerful shudder of revulsion rolled through her. She'd never touched evil before, but she could feel that something very sadistic ran through Margetta's veins.

Willow breathed hard as Axton took her hand. He gripped it hard, squeezing until it hurt, but she couldn't cry out.

"You'll do as you're told, Mistress," Axton said. "I have command of you now, and you will do whatever I say."

Margetta ran a hand down Willow's head and hair. "Axton is going to drink from you now and somewhere in that drinking you'd better choose to bond with him, or he will take you all the way to the grave, do you understand? You bond or you die."

Willow found she could move her eyes, the only thing that worked in the stasis spell. She shifted her gaze to the illuminated wraith-fae who smelled sickly sweet. She tried to speak, but couldn't.

Margetta narrowed her gaze and waved her hand once more. "You may speak."

Willow gasped at the sudden freeing of her vocal chords, then said, "I despise you."

Margetta smiled. "Despise me all you want. Just tell me you understand that I'm giving you the choice of life or death? And answer me, Willow, or I will kill one of your ineffective guards."

Willow glanced at the Guardsmen out the window of her home. All were unaware of the events inside the house. "I understand."

Margetta stepped back. "Axton, this party is all yours and I have other critical business to attend to. Once she bonds, the stasis will end or you can also end it by giving her a solid blow anywhere on her body. Enjoy."

The golden light dissipated and Willow felt the evil presence fade then disappear.

Axton slid his hand up around Willow's neck and held her gaze. "The moment I caught your blood rose scent the other night, I made a vow to myself that I'd make you mine." He leaned close and sniffed her throat.

The part of Willow that was a blood rose failed to differentiate even a little bit between Axton and Malik. Her heart thrummed heavily now, while her body created an excess of rich blood intended to ease the suffering of any mastyr, whether good or evil.

His fangs descended.

~ ~ ~

Sweat poured off Malik's brow. He'd never worked so hard in his life as he strove to find a way out of the trap that had been laid for him. His heart beat hard and every muscle in his body ached with the effort to try to move. But all he'd succeeded in doing was flexing to the point of causing more than one muscle to cramp painfully.

As a man used to fighting, of doing battle with either the energy from his palms or his fists, being held in stasis was nothing less than torture.

He forced himself to take a few deep breaths and calm down. There had to be a way out.

Willow. Sweet Goddess, what was happening to her right now? He tried to reach for her telepathically, but couldn't.

He then searched through each of his frequencies, including both his mating frequency and his battle vibration but nothing had the smallest effect on the stasis. And he still couldn't reach anyone beyond the spell that had bound him.

When a new wave of dizziness hit him, he would have fallen had the spell not held him upright.

A golden light suddenly filled the entryway, and a very beautiful woman appeared. Yet he knew without having to be told that he was looking at the Ancient Fae, the woman responsible for centuries of anguish in every realm of his world.

Margetta, a wraith-fae of enormous power who worked in tandem with her husband, Gustave, had discovered how to forge a bond between wraiths and any other realm-folk. These bonds created violent fighting teams that Margetta was presently using in an attempt to take over the Nine Realms.

Malik thought back to Davido's warning that the entire fate of their world depended on what happened right now in his realm.

"How are you, Mastyr Malik?" For someone so evil, she had a voice that sounded of soft wind chimes, but he wasn't about to be drawn in.

She waved a hand. "You may speak."

"Fuck you, Margetta."

She clucked her tongue, tsking at him. The bitch. "Is that anyway to talk to the woman who holds your life in her hands? But I do have something I need to tell you and though it gives me great joy, you probably won't like it. I just wanted you to know that I've brought my army into your realm, and I'll shortly begin my invasion of the wraith colony."

In his effort to separate from Willow, he knew he'd just brought disaster down on his realm.

"And again, fuck you."

She narrowed her eyes slightly. "Well, for that little piece of insolence, I am going to have kill you. But don't worry, I'll do it slow, that way you'll have the illusion you can escape. And while you're breathing your last, Axton will take Willow for his own and the power they will create together will change the future of the Nine Realms forever, make no mistake."

She laughed this time, and the tips of her wraith-fangs showed. She waved her arm and a wave hit him, this time of terrible pain.

But when it passed, he was left with what felt like an invisible band around his chest.

She watched him carefully, smiling all the while.

He took a deep breath, ready to shout her down, but the band tightened into a vise, and with each breath that followed, it tightened a little more.

Margetta had cast a spell that would slowly suffocate him.

Mentally, he cursed long and loud but worked to draw as little air into his lungs as possible, yet with each breath he felt the band cinch.

Without the ability to reach out for help, or to move, or to stop the band-spell, he knew he was going to die.

His spirit caved within him and again, if he hadn't been held in stasis, he would have fallen to his knees.

Margetta drew close and touched his face. "You're one of the most handsome men I've ever seen. I can end this agony you're suffering if you'll agree to be with me, to share my bed."

"I'd rather be dead." The band tightened some more.

She waved her hand again. "And now no more talking and I definitely don't want you calling out for help."

He tried to answer her, but the paralysis had returned to his vocal chords.

"I wish I could stay, Mastyr, because it would give me great pleasure to watch you breathe your last, but I really do need to coordinate my wraith-pairs. They're hopeless without me." She lifted an arm and vanished.

Another breath. Another tightening of the band.

He thought of Willow caught in Axton's trap and how he'd failed to protect her. Why hadn't it occurred to him that Axton would make Willow his priority instead of the wraith colony?

He trembled head-to-foot at the thought of another vampire feeding from Willow and the woman that belonged to him. He would always think of her as his.

Then a thought even worse surfaced. Axton would bond with the woman *Malik loved.*

His chest ached as though he'd just been punched hard right over his heart. Why hadn't he seen the truth sooner about what Willow was to him?

He understood now that she wasn't just his blood rose. Somewhere during all those months of chasing her, she'd gotten under his skin.

And he loved her.

But as the bands tightened and full-on suffocation drew close, he had to admit another horrible truth. He wouldn't even be in this mess if he hadn't been in such a Goddess be-damned hurry to leave Willow.

He could see the signs now that Margetta had been after her. Willow had complained of headaches and she hadn't slept well all night. A fae as powerful as Willow could have self-healed easily, but he'd been intent on creating some distance, and now here he was having fallen into Margetta's trap.

He felt like five kinds of fool. Alexandra the Bad had called it right when she kept slapping at his chest and calling him a stupid man, because right now that's exactly what he was. He'd been lying to himself and calling it smart.

With barely any air now flowing into his lungs, his arrogance left him. What remained was humility and the truth that if given the chance, he'd bond with her and not think twice about it.

This time, a new dizziness came over him, because his brain was slowly being deprived of oxygen.

The whole situation lay before him from the time Axton had begun his attacks on the entrance to the wraith colony until this moment. What struck him was that he no longer worked alone but had functioned as part of a team, whether with Alexandra and the fae leadership, or with Zane and his Guard, or with Willow.

He felt in his bones that his going-it-alone days were gone. He saw a new future of greater cooperation all over his realm and that was when he realized he'd forgotten one of the vibrations that he and Willow had tapped into.

The earth itself.

But could he reach this most primal frequency so far away from the wraith colony?

He had no idea, but he had to try.

With black spots coming and going in front of his eyes, he opened to the gift Willow had given him of the ability to feel the power of the Nine Realms itself as it lay deep in the earth.

He drew the vibrations up into his body and felt the frequency begin to push back against Margetta's spell.

Magically, the bands loosened enough for him to start gasping in air. With each breath, the spots before his eyes lessened, and the bands stretched wide until finally the band-spell broke.

Unfortunately, the stasis spell still held, but he relaxed and kept the earth's vibration moving through his body. This time, he reached out to Alexandra the Bad and discovered she was right outside his door. He could feel her there, but he still couldn't reach her telepathically or move a muscle.

With a new-found conviction that he would only save Ashleaf by including everyone, he kept aiming the earth-vibration in Alexandra's direction until could he actually feel her reaching back toward him.

Something was happening.

Something good.

He pressed harder and now he could feel her telepathic frequency through the door.

So close. Almost there.

He put on one last, strong effort and the moment he connected with Alexandra, a white light exploded all around him and the stasis spell dissolved.

He whirled toward the door and jerked it open.

"Thank the Goddess you're alive," she shouted. "I could feel you were almost gone!"

He'd never been so grateful to see anyone in his entire life as Alexandra, and behind her the remaining fae leadership.

He moved swiftly and caught her up in a gigantic hug, whirling her in a circle until she was slapping at his arms. "Put me down! Your woman is near death, idiot."

He almost took off, but he remembered his hard-earned lesson. Turning to her, he said, "Please, you must come with me. All of you."

Alexandra looked almost thunderstruck. "Of course we will, and you are learning at last."

"I hope to the Goddess I am."

As he took to the skies, the fae with him, he contacted Zane, pathing, *Get all our forces, including the Troll Brigade over to the entrance to the colony. Margetta and her army are about to attack.*

~ ~ ~

Willow wept.

Her body and soul felt ripped into two pieces. One part of her craved the heinous vampire that drank her down and the other tried to find some way out.

Axton hurt her where he sucked heavily at her neck. He was strong like Malik and held her trapped in his arms. She still couldn't move because of the stasis. She found it hard to breathe.

She tried to access her vine-power, thinking she could bring the vines close and tie him up. But the vines merely hovered a few inches away, apparently torn to act because she was equally torn.

So her vine power was of no use and each drop of blood Axton took powered him more and more, while draining her of strength.

And still she craved him as a blood rose to his mastyr status, needing to bond with him.

As she reached the point of having to choose between death or bonding with a madman, she wondered how she'd gotten into such a terrible predicament. Until now, she and Malik had stuck close to each other in order to keep this very thing from happening.

But Malik had left because of his need to get back to his men.

And she'd let him go.

Now she was here, unable to move and hardly able to breathe and so close to surrendering to her cravings for Axton, that she trembled head-to foot.

As her tears flowed, however, what began to rise up within her was a kind of rage she'd never experienced before, or perhaps never allowed herself to feel.

Throughout most of her life, everything that happened outside of her control had dictated her path, swallowing up her will and her belief in self-direction.

But why was she always at the mercy of the willfulness of others or of events she couldn't control like the deaths of her parents or the arrival of a supernatural gift she'd never asked for?

Maybe the fault lay within her, and just maybe she'd accepted things far too easily and given up her right to vote. She thought about what was within her control: the vines, her ability to connect with the earth, her telepathy, and her connection with Malik and the five powerful fae.

She'd tried reaching out to Malik, but he hadn't responded to her efforts.

As Axton's mating vibration flowed over hers, spiking her need to bond with him, something within her refused to acquiesce. From this point forward, she would have a say in her life's path and right now that meant refusing to bond with Axton, despite her almost overpowering cravings for him.

She realized that this would mean her death, but it would be far worse to be bonded with such a monster.

The moment she made the decision, she felt his mating vibration retreat as though seriously rebuffed.

But he didn't seem to care. He merely squeezed her tighter and pathed, *Then death it is, Willow, which is for the best, since I can smell the wraith on you.*

Axton hated wraiths and half-breeds with a passion, even though he pretended otherwise during all his PR moments. That he'd joined forces with Margetta, a wraith-fae, was the absolute height of hypocrisy.

Well guess what, she responded, *I've learned at the knee of two of the oldest wraiths in our world that we're all descended from the first wraith our Creator made. That's right. Even you are part wraith.*

He drew back, his eyes blistered with rage. "You fucking bitch. How dare you say something like that to me?"

She couldn't believe he'd stopped drinking, which was a big mistake. The second mistake was that he raised his arm and back-handed her hard so that she flew across the room, hitting the living room floor and slamming into the wall by the door.

He must have forgotten that Margetta had told him that a solid blow would break the spell.

And it did.

Willow didn't hesitate, but ordered the vines nearest him to attack. They instantly surrounded every part of his body, whipping his arms close to his sides and sealing his legs together. "What the hell?"

She knew a strong impulse to go to the kitchen, grab one of her sharpest blades, and end his sorry life. But there was so much more at stake than her own need for revenge.

But she didn't think it would hurt to toy with the bastard a little.

She went to the kitchen, found her butcher knife, then and returned. The vines responded to her intent by creating an opening across his throat just below his Adam's apple.

"What are you doing?" His eyes were wild as he stared down at the knife. "Don't. Please, don't."

"You're begging me? Why just a minute ago you were drinking me to death and happy to do it."

She pressed the blade against Axton's throat and the bastard screamed like a little girl.

A hand caught her wrist. "Don't Willow, we need this asshole."

Malik.

Her heart did three quick cartwheels.

She glanced up at him, but turned just enough to wink at him. "Give me one good reason why I shouldn't cut him ear-to-ear."

Malik picked up her cue. "Because he has the information we need to deliver up the name of every member of The Society."

"It won't help you now," Axton spat.

"Why's that?" Willow asked.

"Because Margetta's already inside the colony taking her prize. Ashleaf won't last long now."

Once more, she pressed the knife to his throat. "Listen up, Axton. I don't care how many names you have. I'm the one with the blade in my hand and the power of the vines and I will cut your throat open if I have to."

His eyes widened, but he shifted his gaze to Malik. "You won't get a single name if she kills me."

Willow shifted slightly and met Malik's gaze. He wore a half-smile on his lips as he crossed his arms over his chest. "You know what? Have at him, Willow. This is your party right now and I'll back your play. Kill the bastard."

Once more he begged. "What do you want, Mistress? I'll give you anything you want."

She eased the blade back. "That's better. So here it is. I want to know how and where Margetta is going to attack, especially if she's got some kind of spell going on. And since you've said she's already inside the colony, I want the exact location." Just for emphasis, she cut him just off to the side of his vein."

He yelped once more and sweat poured down his face.

"She's at the northernmost end of the colony. She gave a new charm to one of my men and he was able to break through while you were held in stasis."

Willow narrowed her eyes. "I just have one question. Why did she even need your help? She's got so much power all on her own."

"Because she's a wraith, that's why. Something about the colony wouldn't let her act directly against your shield. I don't understand it myself. Wraiths aren't anxious to hurt their own kind though they love enslaving others. A real paradox, don't you think?"

Willow didn't think she could despise anyone as much as she did Axton.

Turning to Malik, she nodded to him.

~ ~ ~

Malik barked his first order. "We head to the colony entrance now."

He held out his arm for Willow, but she stunned him by shaking her head. "There might be a better way."

"I need to get my men in there."

He felt wild with desperation, but Willow put a hand on his arm. "I've come to a couple of decisions, and we need to tend to each of them first."

He glanced at Alexandra who was frowning at him, her brows forming the usual porcupine quills again. She shook her head and he watched her shape the words, 'stupid man', on her lips.

He put a hand to his head. "Sweet Goddess, I'm an idiot."

Alexandra nodded, but smiled as she said, "You're learning."

He settled his warrior bristles and stepped back just enough to better encompass all five fae. To Willow, he said, "What's the first decision?"

"I'm removing the protective shield. That way your men can get in right now and go to work."

"I didn't even think about the shield." He glanced at Alexandra. "What's your take on this?"

"That Willow is in charge of the colony as well as the shield, and I trust her judgment."

Malik nodded, trying to get used to being part of a larger realm team. He turned to Willow. "But you said a couple of decisions?"

She nodded, then smiled, a blush suffusing her cheeks. "You and I need to bond, right now. I know it in my gut. Besides, I'm in love with you and have been for a gremlin's age."

As a profession of love, Malik wasn't sure he'd heard anything better in his life. He moved into her and even with Axton still struggling in the vines, he took her in his arms. "But, Willow, what about my part in your father's death?"

Tears filled her eyes. "I know you, Malik. I've always believed in you. You're forgiven, do you hear me? Forgiven."

Something like breaking glass shattered inside his chest, his heart, his soul. He'd been held prisoner by his work, by his guilt over all the half-breed deaths, by being so alone. Now here was Willow, this enormous miracle in his life, forgiving him for the unforgivable."

He kissed her. "I love you, Willow. I'm so sorry for holding back and for leaving you the way I did. It was incredibly foolish."

She caressed his cheek. "But I let you go even though I knew I was vulnerable."

"All right you two," Alexandra chimed in. "You have time for this later. We've got wraiths to save. Get the bond done and let's get moving."

Malik nodded briskly. "You're right."

He held Willow's gaze. "I give my heart to you and my will. I accept this bond with every ounce of my being."

Willow's smile softened. "And I bond with you, Malik of Ashleaf Realm."

He kissed her again and let his mating vibration roar as loud as it wanted to. Her answering vibration was no less as powerful and the two frequencies flowed toward each other, intertwined, then just like that, locked into place.

Malik had thought it would take some time, but they were both ready and the bond sealed up fast.

Willow drew back, a hand on her chest. "That was amazing."

"It was. It is." He smiled. "Now how about we go save our wraiths."

"First, let me lose the shield over the wraith colony."

"I'll contact both Zane and Evan to let them know what's happening." As he watched Willow close her eyes and felt an almost overwhelming vibration fill the entire living space, he tapped Zane's telepathic frequency.

It's all quiet here, Malik.

Not for long. I've got Axton bound up at Willow's treehouse, but Margetta's in the colony, at the northern end. Seems you were right. Margetta was working with Axton only she's got her army with her. Willow just removed the protective shield so that you can take our combined forces into battle. Can you see anything yet?

Damn. Look at that. I can see the entire colony below me now. All right, I'm on it.

I'll be heading in your direction in just a few minutes.

Malik shut down his telepathy and turned to Willow. "Zane and his men are headed in."

Axton barked his laughter. "It won't do you any good. Margetta has a bigger army than you can imagine."

"Shut the fuck up," Malik countered.

Willow jerked her head in Axton's direction. "But what do we do with him while we're gone?"

"I've got this." He moved to the front door and signaled for Willow's security detail to come in.

The Guardsmen were stunned to find Axton inside the main treehouse. Before any of them could express their dismay, Malik explained that Margetta had shielded their ability to see Axton and not to worry. He then ordered them to take him to prison and guard him.

"What about the vines?" the squad leader asked.

"Right," Willow said. She stepped forward and passed her hand over the mass connected to Axton, severing them. The ones wrapped around Axton remained where they were, holding him tight.

"Don't worry," Willow said. "The vines are strong and you can use them to haul him away. They'll hold until you want them removed."

With that, the vampires flipped Axton horizontal. When he protested, one of them did what Malik wished he could have done and brought the heel of his boot down on Axton's face.

The vampire spouted blood from his nose and moaned, but made no more protests. Once they had him outside, they flew him into the air.

Willow shook her head. "I don't think I'll be easy until I hear back that he's incarcerated."

"I'm with you on that."

As Malik glanced from the five fae to Willow, he didn't err a second time, but asked all of them, "How should we proceed?"

Willow slid her arm around his waist and hopped onto his booted foot. "Let's get to the colony now, all of us. I have a powerful feeling we'll be needed soon."

Malik took to the air with Willow pinned to his side. The bond had increased his sensitivity to her so that he could feel her almost warrior-like intensity to be heading into battle. *You ready for this?* he asked.

I am.

Holding Willow close, he flew with the leaders of the Fae Guild north to the battle site. Everyone had grown quiet and focused, the same way his Vampire Guard or Troll Brigade would be if headed for a major conflict.

Nearing the coordinates that Axton had supplied, Malik began to slow and all five women stayed within a few feet of each other, matching his speed. He saw his Vampire Guard, along with Zane's, battling in the distance against a huge number of Invictus wraith-pairs. Blue flashes of hand-blast energy clashed with answering red flashes, the latter color belonging exclusively to the deadly wraith-pairs.

Most of the fighting took place in the air, which meant that the injured fell to the forested ground below. But even in the air, he could see the Troll brigade move in swiftly along the forest paths to secure the enemy.

But it was the shrieking of the wraiths that hurt his sensitive vampire hearing, a sound designed to frighten their opposition.

He drew to a stop, hovering in the air three hundred yards from the nearest conflict.

Alexandra the Bad drew close. "I've never seen anything like this."

"If you and your fae sisters need to leave, I understand."

"Not on your life, but thank you for the thought. We're here to support you and to support Willow. We'll see this through. We're all citizens of the Nine Realms and that bitch needs to be stopped."

Malik itched to join the physical fighting as well. He could see Zane in the distance battling three pairs at once and looking righteously powerful as his blue shield held against all kinds of physical weapons. But one by one, his assailants fell to the earth.

Glancing once more into the forest, he saw his Troll Brigade move with great care as they bound up any surviving wraith-pairs. Zane would have had them killed outright, but Malik wanted Samantha of Bergisson Realm to have a chance at rehabilitating as many as possible. The bonded realm-person, usually taken against his or her will, deserved a chance at being restored to normal realm life. Those bonded to wraiths were enslaved to the wraith without the ability to fight that bond.

Because Malik could see that the combined forces would be victorious, he started to relax.

But at that moment, the entire northern section lit up in a golden glow and he knew exactly what it meant.

"Shit."

"Oh, no," Willow murmured. "Margetta's got at least another two hundred wraith-pairs with her. Our forces will be overwhelmed."

"Unfortunately, you're exactly right."

As the additional wraith-pairs entered the battlefield in the air, Zane shouted for a retreat, something Malik would have done as well. They needed to regroup.

But the Invictus, under Margetta's direction, swept after the retreating Guardsmen and forced engagement.

Malik knew they'd be wiped out if something wasn't done.

His warrior instinct was to take off and join the fray. But his recent bond with Willow as well as his realization that he needed to expand his thinking into much larger teamwork, forced him to hold back.

What was needed was fae power to counteract Margetta. If they could force her to leave the field, her Invictus would be thrown into disarray.

To his team, he said, "Because we're outnumbered, we can't fight a straight up battle. Instead, we need to focus on Margetta. If we can somehow oppose her fae power, we'll have a chance."

"I think you're right," Willow said. The five fae added their agreement.

"Willow, I'm going to release you to levitate on your own. I didn't tell you what happened at my house, but Margetta held me in a spell and I only escaped because of the vibration from the earth. I want you to engage the heartbeat of the Nine Realms right now. I'm convinced that's what will turn the tide of the battle."

She nodded her acquiescence, then slid away from him to levitate easily in the air. Malik encouraged the five fae to form a circle and a moment later all seven joined together in the air by holding hands.

Willow closed her eyes even while levitating.

And just like that, he felt the vibration from the earth travel through the night sky, passing through his body and Willow's. The same powerful frequency then sped quickly through the five fae.

As the waves began an outward progression, Margetta's golden light wavered. She must have understood the danger, because she headed straight for them.

"Looks like the Ancient Fae is worried," he said.

Willow nodded. "But even if she draws close, don't pay her any attention. She won't be able to touch us."

Margetta had assumed her wraith-form and arrived with a shriek louder and more piercing than anything he'd heard before. Willow's hand clamped around his as did the fae to his left.

The Fae Guild women began to chant and the earth's power flowed.

Margetta made sweeping passes overhead. She threw red arcs of battle energy in their direction, trying to disrupt them. But Willow was right; they couldn't be touched, not joined as they were with one intent, one purpose.

The frequency rumbled from deep in the earth as it poured through Willow and afterward through them all. Waves of energy pulsed now, stronger and stronger.

A white light began to glow around them which caused Margetta to utter a shriek of anguish and afterward to fly swiftly in a northern direction. He could see she was panicked, which gave him tremendous hope.

"Keep streaming, Willow, no matter what happens." The battle still raged, but Vojalie's earlier vision swept through his mind of an explosion of white light. And as Margetta began to withdraw her troops, he added, "Prepare for the impossible."

Willow turned and held his gaze. She seemed to understand because she smiled. He met Alexandra's gaze, then each of her sister-fae in turn. A group understanding travelled among them all and as one they flew in the direction of the battle. The vibration from the heart of the Nine Realms stayed right with them and continued to increase in speed and power.

Malik shook from the adrenaline and the vibration.

The fae chanted once more, Willow with them.

The chanting grew louder and as they reached the periphery of the battle their joined energy began to flow outward faster and faster. As that energy reached successive battling pairs, every warrior, whether vampire or Invictus, suddenly ceased all movement except levitation.

On they moved in Margetta's direction, passing to the center of the battlefield. Each time they drew close to an Invictus pair, stasis occurred again.

Margetta shrieked louder, calling for her army to come to her. A great number of them rushed to her side as she ushered them into the north. She shrieked and shouted.

But Malik's team grew stronger, the power flowing heavily until suddenly, the power erupted into a ball of pure white energy, flashing through the night sky and encompassing the Vampire Guard, the Troll Brigade on the ground, and all the remaining Invictus pairs. The white energy rolled, exploding in waves over and over, rushing through him, through Willow and through the five fae.

Chills chased over him and his heart pounded. The Nine Realms was a land of frequencies and this one that emerged from the heart of all the realms felt like love and power combined. He slid his arm around Willow's waist and drew her closer to him, wanting to share the moment with her.

As waves of white light kept moving and exploding, he held her gaze.

Her beautiful hazel eyes were filled with tears and great happiness. "We've saved the wraiths."

He nodded. "Hell, yeah, we did!"

Alexandra the Bad called to him. "Kiss her, warrior. It will do you both a lot of good and heal three centuries of your desperate solitude."

He didn't need to hear the advice twice and as the cyclone of magnificent power surrounded them all, he drew his bonded blood rose into this arms and kissed her. Willow melted against him so that he could feel her heart beating in rhythm to the flow of the white waves. *I love you, Willow, with all my heart.*

He heard a soft coo leave her throat as he deepened his kiss, his tongue making promises for a later joining. She slid her arms around his neck. Her words flowed through his mind, *You will always have my heart, Mastyr.*

He kissed her deeper still, wrapping his arms tightly around her, holding her as close as he could. He wanted her to feel all that was in his heart.

When at last he drew back, the heart of the Nine Realms began to recall her power, and the white waves slowly eased back.

With one arm still holding Willow close, he glanced around and saw that Margetta was gone as well as a large portion of her army.

The fighting had ended, and Zane had already taken charge.

The explosion had rendered the remaining Invictus wraith-pairs harmless so that both the Vampire Guard and the Troll Brigade were binding up the pairs that Margetta had failed to take with her.

What went through his mind was that he would never have believed that chasing Willow through the forest repeatedly would have led him to this moment of being bound to her and working with the Fae Guild leaders to defeat Margetta. He knew his experience had been different, and that no other mastyr or a bonded blood rose had been able to connect to the heart of the Nine Realms as he and Willow had. Maybe they were unique in that way. He wasn't sure.

Regardless, he felt humbled and grateful that he'd been able to be part of resolving an impossible situation. He thanked each of the fae for joining with him and Willow, and he especially thanked Alexandra for encouraging him not to be stupid.

Finally, he turned to Willow and despite the fact that he had an audience he kissed her again, letting her know in this way just how much she meant to him.

Because of the bond, he could feel the warmth of her response and what his arms felt like surrounding her. She, too, was full of gratitude.

~ ~ ~

Willow continued to hold within her bones the latent vibration that had come from the earth and resulted in the stunning explosion of light and power and warmth that had enveloped the entire team. She felt changed and so full within her spirit that she could barely form a proper string of thoughts. She savored the feel of Malik's arms around her, the sensation of his tongue pulsing within her mouth, the strength of his Guardsman body.

She loved him with every particle of her fae-wraith spirit.

She loved him.

Still, no words would come, so she let him feel her love with the pressure of her hands surrounding his back, with her hips connected to him and with all that she was. She desired more than anything to be joined to him once more in her treehouse bedroom with the vines surrounding them both.

When he finally drew back, she nodded and the words emerged from her at last. "I love you, Malik."

"You have my heart."

The next hour became a blur of sticking close to Malik, of watching the warriors take their prisoners away, of receiving thanks from so many of the Guardsmen for the white light explosion that had ended the battle and saved hundreds of warrior lives.

She remained in a completely euphoric state from all that had happened.

As for Malik, he never once relinquished her hand except to slide an arm around her waist and keep her close. Maybe he sensed that she needed to be near him or maybe he felt the same way. They were bonded now, a mastyr to his blood rose.

Eventually, they landed at Illiandra and Gervassay's villa where a great deal of champagne flowed and more gratitude poured from every quarter.

But like a bride on her honeymoon, she needed to be alone and joined to her man. He must have understood, because he slowly began leading her through the room and bidding everyone farewell.

At last outside, and with the shield temporarily disabled, he simply took Willow up into the air and flew her swiftly to her treehouse.

No words were necessary as he dropped down on the platform outside her bedroom. She moved within and began stripping out of her clothes, letting each garment fall to the floor on her way to the shower.

Malik wasn't far behind and if the stall hadn't been undersized he would have joined her beneath the spray.

As he took his turn in her way-too-small shower, she stuck close and didn't exactly get dried off before he was plastered against her.

Eventually he carried her to the bed.

The vines moved in swiftly so that as soon as he entered her, the tendrils, leaves, and stems bound them in the most extraordinary cocoon.

Malik moved in a steady rhythm, driving in and out. All the while, he kissed her forehead, her temple, her cheek and sucked on the sensitive tip of her ear until she was close to ecstasy.

He nudged her neck aside and at the same time presented his wrist to her. She bit and began to suck. A moment later, his fangs struck, sending a delicious shard of pleasure through her abdomen. He drank from her throat and moaned heavily, his hips working her up until she breathed raggedly through her nose.

His blood powered her in the same way that she could feel just how much her life-force fed and strengthened him.

He added a vibration to his cock and began to move faster. Her breathing grew erratic and because she was so close, she released his wrist and cried out. He left her throat as well and the vines shifted to accommodate their movements then bound them once more.

She barely felt grounded as he quickened his pace.

Holding her gaze, he said, "I love you, Willow, with everything that is in me."

"Malik. Oh, sweet Goddess, Malik!"

He understood and moved vampire fast. She flew quickly over the edge, pleasure streaking through her in strong pulses. Her abdomen tightened and ecstasy flowed in a swell of sensation up through her chest, surrounding her heart, then swiftly pounding through her mind.

Malik roared wildly as he came.

The vines writhed all around her, adding sensation on sensation.

The orgasm kept coming in heavy waves until she was screaming and stars once more filled her mind.

Love was what followed, exquisite pure love that felt just like the white light from the heartbeat of the Nine Realms.

Did she hear music? Was the earth singing? Or the Goddess? Or the heartbeat itself?

"Open your eyes Willow."

When had she shut them?

Malik lay relaxed on top of her and caressed her face as he kissed her. His smile was so tender that her heart began to ache. Gone was the sadness that had cloaked him for decades.

"I wish I could express just how much you've changed everything for me, Willow. Everything."

She understood. "And you've done the same for me. I never thought to have love in my life because of my duty to the colony. Now you're here, sharing my bed. I'm overwhelmed with joy and with the wonder of it all."

"Me, too."

He kissed her again and again, and because he was still inside her, he grew very firm once more.

He made love to her well past even the breach of dawn so that as the night-birds took to their nests and the day birds set up their own peculiar racket, she added her own cries to the wild cacophony.

Later, she cast her charm and built a barrier to all the noise so that she could fall asleep in Malik's arms.

And she dreamed the dreams of the Nine Realms, of one day all the realms being free of Margetta and the Invictus.

~ ~ ~

The next night, at full-dark, Malik sat with Zane on Willow's meditation porch drinking a couple of beers. Zane would be taking his men home in a few minutes, but wanted a word with Malik.

"So you're bonded now."

Malik smiled. "Yep."

"I won't ask what it's like because you've got so much feel-good glowing from you right now that I'm getting a sunburn."

Malik swigged his beer and watched the bats float in and out of the branches, moving in their erratic yet smooth way. "I never thought it could be like this."

Zane groaned. "I've heard that more than once, so, shit." His deep voice rolled through the forest. He touched the dagger tattoo on the side of his neck, rubbing as though in pain.

Malik glanced at him. There was nothing he could say, but he saw the dark look in Zane's eye and knew exactly what that felt like as well. The storm would come to Swanicott Realm as it had come to the others, bearing hurricane force winds with nothing to be done except to face Margetta and stand tall.

So, for Zane's sake, he kept silent.

Zane finished his beer and finally bid farewell, taking off into the night, his Guardsman coat flapping behind him.

Malik disposed of the empty bottles, then went on a hunt for Willow.

He found her below her treehouse complex, near the stream, pulling weeds in her vegetable garden. "I saw Zane leave."

Malik nodded. "He's taking his men home."

"Thought as much. We have a new realm here, don't we?"

Despite her garden gloves, he pulled her into his arms, nuzzling her neck. She moaned softly in return.

"How about a swim?" he asked.

"You mean in my secret pool?"

"I want to feel the waves wash over us again."

She drew back and planted her hand on his chest. "And you're sure you won't be needed the rest of the night?"

He shook his head. "Evan has everything in hand. Besides, Alexandra the Bad told me I'd be in for a world of hurt if I didn't tend to you over the next several nights as my one and only mission."

She slid her hands into his hair and dislodged his Guardsman clasp. "I think Alexandra is the smartest woman alive."

Malik smiled then suggested she lose the gloves. She whipped them off, afterward holding her arms open for him, ready to fly.

He drew her tight against his waist and after kissing her, rose into the air.

As he flew her to her favorite pool, he knew without a doubt that he held heaven in his arms.

He thought back to the last chase and couldn't believe all that had happened. Axton could never again trouble his realm and he now had a blood rose, and a profound love he never thought he'd have.

Yes, above all, love had found him at long last, in the wilderness, in the wild, in the arms of a worthy woman.

Thank you for reading EMBRACE THE WILD! In our new digital age, authors rely on readers more than ever to share the word. Here are some things you can do to help!

Sign up for my newsletter! You'll always have the *latest releases, hottest pics*, and *coolest contests*! http://www.carisroane. com/contact-2/

Leave a review! You've probably heard this a lot lately and wondered what the fuss is about. But reviews help your favorite authors -- A LOT -- to become visible to the digital reader. So, anytime you feel moved by a story, leave a short review at your favorite online retailer. And you don't have to be a blogger to do this, just a reader who loves books!

Enter my latest contest! I run contests all the time so be sure to check out my contest page today! **ENTER NOW**! http://www. carisroane.com/contests/

Be sure to check out the Blood Rose Tales – TRAPPED, HUNGER, and SEDUCED -- shorter works set in the world of the Blood Rose, for a quick, satisfying read.
BLOOD ROSE TALES BOX SET
http://www.carisroane.com/blood-rose-tales-box-set/

About the Author

Hi, Everyone! I'm a NY Times Bestselling Author and I write super-sexy paranormal romance fiction designed to be as much an adventure as a soul-satisfying experience. With every book, I try to give a taste of real life, despite the fact that I'm writing about hunky vampire warriors. You'll come away engrossed in the lives of my vampires as they wage war, as they make love, and as they answer the tough questions of life in terms of purpose, eternity, and how to raise a family! I began my career with Kensington Publishing writing Regency Romance as Valerie King. In 2005, Romantic Times Magazine honored me with a career achievement award in Regency Romance. I've published sixteen paranormal stories to-date, some self-published and some for St. Martin's Press. To find out more about me, please visit my website!

www.carisroane.com

Author of

Guardians of Ascension Series – Warriors of the Blood crave the breh-hedden
Dawn of Ascension Series – Militia Warriors battle to save Second Earth
Blood Rose Series – Only a blood rose can fulfill a mastyr vampire's deepest needs
Blood Rose Tales – Short tales of mastyr vampires who hunger to be satisfied
Men in Chains Series – Vampires struggling to get free of their chains and save the world

Other Titles:

CPSIA information can be obtained
at www.ICGtesting.com
Printed in the USA
FSOW02n1104090217
30618FS

9 781512 114348